The Watchmen of the Provincetown Pier

Raphaël L. Marly

Acknowledgment

To you, my dear Mélanie, to you, Rémi, my boy, and to my grandchildren, Marcel and Alba—despite the distance that separates us, from France to Canada.

This book, though tinged with shadows, is also a tribute to our unbreakable bond. May each word remind you that, even when far from one another, love and connection always unite us, and the memories we share continue to brighten our thoughts.

David Sinclair

Appearance: A ruggedly handsome Boston lieutenant in his late 30s to early 40s. He has short, dark hair, sharp blue-gray eyes that hold a perpetual intensity, and a strong jawline shadowed by stubble. His face bears the weary creases of sleepless nights spent chasing truth. He wears a long, dark trench coat often damp from sea spray, a worn button-up shirt, and leather gloves that have seen their share of crime scenes. His presence exudes quiet authority, but a ghostly melancholy lingers in his expression.

Personality: Intelligent, determined, and deeply introspective. Haunted by the cases he couldn't solve, he pursues the truth with relentless tenacity. Though he has a sharp mind and keen intuition, the burden of his discoveries weighs heavily on him. The ocean calls to him in ways he can't quite explain, as if whispering secrets just beyond his grasp.

Clara Voss

Appearance: A striking woman in her early 30s with pale, sea-kissed skin and long, raven-black hair that drapes over her shoulders like flowing ink. Her deep-set green eyes shimmer with unspoken knowledge, and her lips often curve into a knowing half-smile. A distinctive electric-blue spiral tattoo coils beneath her left ear, made of diatom particles and shark blood. She wears a simple dark turtleneck, sturdy boots, and a long coat that billows like a shadow behind her.

Personality: A brilliant researcher obsessed with unraveling the ocean's mysteries, Clara is both scientist and mystic. She is fiercely independent, unafraid of the unknown, and deeply intuitive. Her fascination with maritime legends and strange disappearances leads her into perilous territory, and she embraces the abyss with fearless curiosity. Even in death, her presence lingers—guiding, warning, and whispering from the depths.

Dr. Silenus

Appearance: A gaunt, aging forensic pathologist with a sharp, angular face that resembles a crab washed ashore. He has sunken, piercing eyes behind round, fogged-up glasses. His skin is pallid, almost translucent under dim lighting, and his bony fingers are always gloved in latex. His dark lab coat, perpetually speckled with ink and seawater stains, adds to his eerie presence.

Personality: Cryptic, eccentric, and slightly unsettling. He speaks in riddles, often making poetic or grotesque observations about death. His fascination with decay borders on obsessive, and his morbid curiosity makes others uneasy. He finds beauty in the macabre and treats each autopsy as if deciphering a forgotten language.

Jake Morrow

Appearance: A weathered, albino fisherman with deep-set wrinkles and sharp, storm-gray eyes. His skin, marked by years of salt and wind, carries the scars of long-forgotten battles with the sea. He wears a frayed wool sweater, a battered captain's hat, and a necklace of sperm whale teeth, each carved with runes. His calloused hands are covered in pearly scars, and his gaze rarely meets anyone's eyes—always looking toward the horizon.

Personality: Gruff and deeply superstitious. He speaks in short, cryptic sentences and distrusts outsiders. He believes the ocean remembers every sin committed against it and that its ghosts walk among the living. He knows more than he lets on but refuses to divulge the full truth, warning that some knowledge is best left buried beneath the waves.

Evan Grey

Appearance: A charismatic yet unsettling man in his mid-40s, always impeccably dressed in tailored suits with a moray-skin tie. His slicked-back, dark hair reveals a widow's peak, and his chiseled features give him a devilish charm. His eyes—cold and calculating—betray an ambition that knows no moral restraint. A faint smirk is permanently etched into his lips, as if he's always in on a secret no one else knows.

Personality: A ruthless businessman and manipulator, Evan views the world through the lens of power and profit. He is the type to shake hands while holding a dagger behind his back. He is fascinated by the ocean's mysteries, but only as resources to exploit. His outward charm conceals a sinister intellect, and his involvement in illicit maritime dealings runs deeper than anyone suspects.

Lila Goode

Appearance: A reclusive woman in her late 30s with sunken amber eyes, gaunt cheeks, and long, unkempt auburn hair streaked with silver. She dresses in faded clothes—thick sweaters and long skirts—as if she's always bracing against the cold. Her fingers, delicate but stained with ink, tremble slightly when she speaks. Her voice is low, like a whisper carried by the tide.

Personality: Haunted and deeply introspective, Lila carries the weight of grief and knowledge. She once studied maritime myths and cryptic frequencies but withdrew from society after Clara's disappearance. Now, she is a keeper of forgotten truths, reluctant to share them but unable to turn away those who seek the same knowledge. Her connection to Clara is one of deep sorrow and reverence.

Isaac

Appearance: An old Wampanoag sailor with skin darkened by time and salt, his face a map of deep-cut lines and scars. His thick, graying beard is braided with tiny shells, and his hair, though thinning, is still wild. He wears a patched oilskin coat, tattered from decades of storms, and his left hand is missing two fingers, a price paid to the sea.

Personality: Wise and enigmatic, Isaac is a guardian of forgotten stories and ancient maritime knowledge. He speaks in riddles, cryptic yet profound, and believes in forces older than humanity. Despite his gruff exterior, he has a deep sense of justice and willingly sacrifices himself to protect those who seek the truth. He walks the line between the living and the dead, an old sailor waiting for the tide to carry him home.

Anaïs

Appearance: A solemn, otherworldly child, no older than 12, with seafoam-green eyes that seem to glow in the dark. Her short, curly hair is always damp, and her small frame moves with an eerie grace, as if she's always listening to something unheard. She wears simple, salt-stained clothes—a tattered white dress and an oversized fisherman's coat.

Personality: Mysterious and wise beyond her years, Anaïs carries the burden of knowledge too vast for a child. She speaks in fragmented riddles and often hums strange, melodic tunes that seem to call the waves. Her origins are unclear, but she appears and disappears like a ghost, leaving behind cryptic warnings and forgotten truths. Whether she is entirely human remains a question unanswered.

Contents

Chapter I
The Litanies of the Lost Shore

I. Prelude to the Murmurs of the Sea

Provincetown awakened in the milky twilight of the marine dawn, its wooden frame twisted by centuries of tides. The pilings of the docks, skeletal remains gnawed at the joints by barnacles, exhaled an age-old lament with every caress of the waves. I stood upon them like a tightrope walker of the tides, listening for the call of sunken Atlantises in the splashing of mooring ropes. The shuttered facades hummed legends of shattered prows, their slats beating the funeral rhythm of unfinished farewells. An autumn sky, a Turner canvas smeared with celestial tears, unfurled its opaline clouds in melancholic drapery, indifferent to the muffled sobs rising from the shore.

David Sinclair inhaled the air, thick with salt and silence. His steely gaze, sharpened by urban tempests, scanned the horizon, searching in the fleeting mist for the outline of truth. Flee Boston? he mused, a bitterness like dried seaweed at the corner of his lips. Port cities keep their dead like precious seashells, polished in the hollows of secret coves and offered as tribute to the deities of the murky deep. His coat, soaked with sea spray, clung to his skin like a second conscience, heavy with the wreckage of intimate shipwrecks he had dragged from the underbelly of Back Bay. The wind sketched ephemeral hieroglyphs in the dunes—an alphabet in motion, revealing in filigree the enigma of Clara Voss.

II. The Geography of Shadows

The beach stretched in a weary curve beneath the pale gaze of the lighthouse. Its golden sand was stained with black seaweed, like stigmata. Clara lay in the hollow of a rocky inlet that old sailors called "the cradle of Tethys." A body offered as an oblation to the gods of the deep. Death, clad in its most majestic finery, bore an awe-inspiring aspect. Her long black hair cascaded around her, her lashes adorned with salt droplets shimmering like mica, and her slightly parted lips held one last mystery, sealed in the abyss. David bent down, his heart beating in syncopation with the muffled waves.

"Look at her hands," murmured Dr. Silenus, the forensic pathologist, with the air of a giant crab washed ashore. His latex-gloved fingers delicately brushed Clara's fingers. "Scribe's calluses… She still held a pen when the tide took her." He pointed to her slightly curved right index finger, where the ghostly imprint of a quill remained. David saw, in the flickering shadows, sleepless nights—Clara poring over shipwreckers' grimoires, deciphering the silences between the lines of old logbooks. A sudden fragrance of sandalwood and blue ink drifted into the air, like a fleeting memory of her solitary vigils.

"No trace of violence," continued the coroner, stroking her marble-white nape. "But this symbol…" His trembling finger indicated an electric blue spiral beneath her left ear, a recent tattoo whose swirls seemed to coil around the undercurrents. "The ink contains diatom particles, but also…" He inhaled the wound with unsettling delight, sending a chill through David. "…shark blood. Curious, isn't it? These chimeras of ink and salt…"

The sea lapped gently against the rock, as if cradling her final slumber. David looked toward the lighthouse, its pale light painting fleeting ideograms on the waves. He wondered if these glyphs were messages to tormented souls or mere whims of the mist.

III. The Choir of the Silent

The beach teemed with an eclectic crowd, composed of both the living and the spectral. Esther Blackwood approached, a Valkyrie of forgotten archives, her sea-green eyes probing the horizon like abyssal scanners. "She was searching for fractures in time, Lieutenant. The cracks where unsettling truths sink and vanish." Her gloved fingers, black lace stained with ink, brushed Clara's notebook with funereal tenderness.

Behind her, Jake Morrow fiddled with a necklace of sperm whale teeth, an albino fisherman with palms etched by pearly scars. His gaze avoided the body, fixed instead on the horizon, as if awaiting a vengeful tide. "Clara asked too many questions," he grumbled, grinding out a cigarette against the rotting wood. "The sea doesn't like it when you rummage through its pockets." A seagull shrieked, tearing the silence with its scaly laughter.

Reverend Ezekiel then emerged from the mist, his black cassock snapping in the wind like a pirate's flag. "The wrath of the Sea Lords befalls the desecrators!" he thundered, brandishing a Bible bound in stingray skin, its cover gleaming with an eerie sheen. His bloodshot eyes locked onto David like a predator's. "Read Ezekiel 26:19! The daughters with gills beneath their shoulder blades have vanished for eternity!"

IV. The Archipelago of Drowned Truths

Clara's room exuded the melancholy of an abandoned museum. David opened Notebook No. 17, bound in "chimera leather," according to Dr. Silenus. The marine ink seemed to ripple on the pages, warped by humidity:

October 13. Meet old Finn at the Drunken Boat. His stories of sirens—seaweed hair, storm voices—oddly match the depositions from the Hawthorne trial (1893). Metaphor or confession? The birth registry mentions "epidermal anomalies" in Morrow's daughters…

October 17. The whaling company archives lie by omission. What were they hiding in those expeditions south of Stellwagen Bank? Why were the harpooners' names erased? A 1922 letter found: "The depths have returned their due." What due?

A photograph slipped from the notebook—a sepia image of weathered sailors on a ship's deck, their faces carved by the wind.

On the back, a scrawled note: "They know. They've always known."

Pinned to the walls, dozens of nautical maps formed a tapestry of disappearances. Each red pin marked a place where women had vanished, their names erased from the records, like graffiti scrubbed from stone. The red lines connecting the points created a haunting visual—a macabre choreography where each pin was a stifled sigh, each thread a choked sob.

V. Nocturne Beneath the Tide's Shadows

Night fell in ribbons of liquid tar, swallowing the last crimson reflections of sunset. David wandered the deserted alleys, listening to the houses whispering their secrets through the cracks in their shutters. Near the lighthouse, he caught sight of figures exchanging wax-cloth-wrapped bundles—sealed missives or condemned evidence?

Midnight tolled at Saint Peter-of-the-Waves. In a dune hollow, he found a half-burned notebook: "They threatened me." The lighthouse only illuminates what it's allowed to see. Ask Jake about his 1995 sighting near the reefs… The rest was lost to ash.

By dawn, the tempestuous sky had erased everything. Only one thing remained, nailed to the police station door—a fragment of a sea chart, marked in blood-red ink: "Search where the whales go to die."

VI. Epilogue: The Song of the Depths

David sat on the dune, watching the gulls trace anxious circles in the leaden sky. In his bag, Clara's notebooks weighed like tombstones. He understood then that truth was not a fish to be harpooned but a shifting current—always present, often elusive.
The ocean grinned back at him, foaming with all the words never spoken. Names and dates were meaningless—the dead of Provincetown guarded a secret older than the cliffs, a mystery stitched into the waves since the dawn of time.
As he rose, he felt the scrutinizing gaze of the deep upon his neck. The sea called him to dive, to dance with the shadows of the Great Forgotten. Whether he wanted to or not, he was now one of the Watchers of Cape Cod, condemned to probe the darkness in search of truths long swallowed by the tide.

Chapter I: Compendium

David Sinclair, a lieutenant from Boston, investigates the mysterious death of Clara Voss, found on a beach in Provincetown with a spiral tattoo beneath her ear. Her journals reveal research into the disappearances of women linked to maritime legends. As David delves deeper, he uncovers a web of secrets involving local figures—Dr. Silenus, Jake Morrow, and Reverend Ezekiel—and nautical maps marked with traces of long-buried crimes.

Chapter II
The Whispers of the Abyss

I. The Dawn of the Shipwrecks

Provincetown awoke in a watercolor light, its outlines blurred by the morning mist. David Sinclair stood at the window of his hotel room, trapped in a dreamlike in-between where the waves inscribed verses onto the sand. The slow, patient surf chanted an elegy for Clara Voss. Each crest of foam was a petal of memory torn from the book of tides, each spray of salt a tear suspended on the curtain of time.

The memory of Clara haunted him—her pearl-like face, eyelids rimmed with salt, hair unfurled in a liquid nocturne. She drifted through his mind like a paradoxical siren—both at peace and tormented by the truths she had pursued. The sea, both accomplice and executioner, rolled its secrets like polished pebbles, indifferent to the tremors of shipwrecked souls.

Morning light filtered through the grimy windows, turning the room into a magic lantern where dust from a suspended world drifted aimlessly. The pale sun gave no warmth, only a sharp clarity that outlined shadows with precision. In them, David saw the ghosts of Provincetown: fishermen with gnarled hands clutching empty bottles, widows whispering prayers at the foot of marine tombstones, and children running along the piers with nets full of melancholy.

II. The Archipelago of Silence

Sheriff O'Neill's office smelled of stale tobacco and damp paperwork. Graham handed over a crumpled sheet, his gesture heavy with implication. "Lila Goode lives near the old abandoned lighthouse. Her tears must have carved channels all the way to the ocean."

The path to Lila's house twisted between fishing shacks with uneven planks, their colors faded by years of salt and regret. Clotheslines snapped in the wind like symbolic hangings while translucent jellyfish—damned souls of the drowned—quivered in the shallow tide pools. Lila's home stood apart, its shutters closed like swollen eyelids. A garden of hollyhocks drooped toward the shore as if waiting for a messenger from the depths.

David knocked. The door creaked open, revealing a ghostly woman with eyes shadowed in ochre.

"Lieutenant Sinclair?" Her voice was as ragged as shells scraped against the reefs.

Inside, the house breathed grief: velvet curtains gnawed by moths, a piano out of tune with yellowed keys, portraits of Clara hung in disorder—her smile frozen before undersea monoliths, her hands clasped over grimoires covered in aquatic runes.

"She studied the songs of right whales," Lila murmured, stroking a silver frame. "She believed their music was a guide to..." A sob twisted her lips. David noticed empty bottles rolling under the couch—a personal shipwreck anchored in the harbor of despair.

III. The Scales of Memory

"This ceremonial mask…" Lila opened a wooden sandalwood chest. The object emerged, carved from a narwhal tusk, inlaid with mother-of-pearl and fossilized shark eyes.

"Clara brought it up from the depths of Stellwagen Bank. She believed it… communicated."

David shivered. The spirals carved into the mask seemed to pulse with the rhythm of the waves.

"Communicated with whom?"

"With those who listen." Her trembling fingers traced a sinuous groove. "The elders spoke of murmurs beneath the storms. Clara recorded sounds… frequencies that tear at the soul." She handed him a notebook covered in musical staves bristling with inhuman peaks.

A breeze slipped through a slightly open window, rustling pages filled with mysterious inscriptions:

"For 30 million years, whales have mourned the loss of their kin. And yet, what do we say?"

"The mask is not an artifact but a mirror."

Lila brushed her fingers over a photo of Clara, radiant on a rock facing the ocean.

"Richard called her a heretic. Evan said she was poisoning Provincetown's soul. But she…" A rough laugh escaped her. "She danced with jellyfish on full moon nights. Claimed she understood their language of poison and light."

IV. The Silt-Stained Interview

Evan's house stood on the cliff, a fortress of glass and steel defying the elements. The mayor welcomed David into an office dominated by a model of his upcoming luxury resort: The Sirens.

"Clara Voss?" He slowly rose and walked to the panoramic window, tracing circles in the air with his finger. "An idealist. She thought the ocean was deeper than our wallets."

David studied the paintings on the walls: Evan shaking golden hands on yachts, his smile strained in front of bulldozers devouring the dunes.

"Her research interfered with your projects?"

A flicker of fury crossed the mayor's gaze.

"She wanted Stellwagen Bank declared a sanctuary! Do you know what a single minute of delay costs on a maritime construction site?"

His voice sank into an abyss, low and vibrating.

"We are not museum keepers, Sinclair. Progress belongs to those who dare drive stakes into the jaws of Poseidon."

Outside, seagulls circled, shrieking their disapproval. David noted Evan's nervous tic—his right hand tapping on a locked drawer. What secrets did that cabinet hold? Contracts tainted with the ink of corruption? Photos of dredges tearing apart the seabed?

V. Nocturne on the Fractures

Night fell like a damp shroud. David walked along the deserted docks, streetlamps casting ghostly halos onto overturned hulls. In the darkness, Provincetown became a theater of shadows: furtive figures exchanging packages near the warehouses, blue glows dancing beneath the pilings, muffled voices carried by the gusts.

He stopped before the abandoned lighthouse. Among the seaweed and rusted beer caps lay a charred notebook. The surviving pages spoke of "cursed frequencies" and "pacts sealed in kelp."

One phrase sent a chill through him:

"They offered me the mask… or perhaps it chose me."

Suddenly, a cry tore through the night—a long wail, half-human, half-marine. David ran toward the beach. Nothing. Only the mocking lapping of the waves. But in the sand, freshly traced, glowed the same spiral patterns as those on the mask…

VI. Epilogue: The Choir of the Deep

Back at the hotel, David spread his notes across the bed. The puzzle pieces fit together like magic:

- The inaudible frequencies Clara recorded
- The mask with its fossilized eyes
- Evan's financial interests
- The disappearances of fishermen noted in old registers

The sea knocked against the windows, insistent. He opened the blackened notebook and discovered a startling sketch: hybrid silhouettes emerging from the waves, arms outstretched toward the mask.

A margin note read:

"The Guardians exist. They are reclaiming what we have stolen."

Somewhere in the night, a solitary whale began to sing—a deep vibration that made the walls tremble.

David understood then: Clara had not drowned. She had been absorbed by a truth too vast for a human body.

He vowed to plunge into these abysses, even if it meant losing his sanity.

Chapter II: Compendium

David delves into Clara's past, captivated by her research on whale songs and marine rituals. He discovers a ceremonial mask and confronts Evan Grey, a corrupt mayor willing to sacrifice the ocean for real estate projects. The underwater frequencies recorded by Clara hint at a disturbing truth lurking in the ocean depths.

Chapter III
The Watery Shadows of Stellwagen

Maritime Matins

Dawn brushed Provincetown with a pearly hand, revealing the scars of the harbor in a new light. The slumbering barges swayed like empty cradles, their oil-streaked hulls weeping iridescent tears. Standing at the threshold of an undiscovered truth, David Sinclair watched the gulls trace anxious parabolas above the settling basins. Their cries slashed through the silence like scalpels, each note screaming the urgency of the still-deaf depths.

His fingers, numb from the damp night air, traced the worn wooden pilings. The warped oak bore the memory of moorings—each gash, a stanza in a criminal poem. At knee height, a fissure shaped like a latitude (42° 03′ N) caught his eye. Suddenly, the spectrometer hanging from his belt, a modern relic, vibrated. Beep-beep. Particles of cesium-137 swirled in the slanted light—an ephemeral constellation betraying the nocturnal passage of Grey Marine's barges. Their phosphorescent wakes, captured by the thermal camera, formed toxic hieroglyphs on the screen.

A peculiar splashing sound drew his attention. In the shadow of Pier 7, where red algae formed a velvet carpet of sludge, and a moon jellyfish pulsed weakly. Its tendrils, streaked with metallic veins, trembled with the rhythm of the waves—antennae attuned to the whispers of the abyss. David saw it as a sign—Clara called them the sentinels of the trenches. With a titanium clamp, he delicately collected a sample, noting how the translucent gel absorbed the light. The creature recoiled, revealing a recurring pattern in its tissues: a stylized octopus logo encircling the letters G.M.C.

"They bear their mark like a stigma," he thought, placing the specimen in a cryogenic tube. Clara's notebook, found three moons ago in a submerged cave, came to mind. Page 19, written feverishly: Jellyfish are the scribes of the ocean—their bodies record every crime.

The Cabinet of Broken Reflections

Lila Goode's house stood like a stranded wreck, its bluish shingles streaked with lichen in the shape of petrified tears. David moved through tufts of sea orache, its heart-shaped leaves quivering in the wind like receptors of anguish. The door groaned on rusted hinges, releasing a breath of air thick with salt and regret.

Inside, it was a museum of mourning. Mirrors veiled in gray tulle reflected fragments of Clara: here, her hand turning the pages of a 19th-century oceanographic grimoire; there, her image trapped in a fishing net hanging from the ceiling. Lila appeared, draped in a gown of nacreous ribbons. "She has been waiting for you for six tides," she murmured, gesturing toward the Edison phonograph, its horn resembling a black metal flower.

On a weathered mahogany table, an open herbarium revealed mutant sargassum. Their swollen vesicles contained a violet liquid that pulsed with the rhythm of David's breath. "Watch," Lila whispered, pouring a drop of acid onto a piece of kelp. The plant bled midnight-blue ink, forming gothic letters: Beneath the sediments, the evidence sleeps.

The phonograph suddenly crackled, spitting out an atonal melody. The needle traced the grooves of a worn wax cylinder, mimicking exactly the tempo of the cannery's oil pumps—78 beats per minute, the crime's sonic signature. David pulled out his digital recorder. The frequency overlay revealed a hidden message: Seek the electric eels of Reservoir B-12.

The Scriptorium of Shadows

Woods Hole University opened its sweating stone entrails. In Richard Davenport's office, science had decayed into cursed alchemy. Formalin-filled vials, lined up like soldiers, contained unspeakable horrors:

A porpoise fetus with eyes replaced by miniature cameras

A giant squid whose suction cups bore barcodes

A colony of genetically modified diatoms designed to absorb benzene

"You mistake progress for desecration!" Richard thundered as the chromatograph scanned lead levels 200 times above the legal limit. David didn't flinch. With a swift motion, he tore down a tapestry depicting Poseidon. Behind it, a reinforced safe spewed out stacks of documents—illegal fishing contracts, falsified pollution reports, and photos of Clara in a diving suit in front of an outfall spewing black torrents.

On a yellowed label, a handwritten note sent chills down David's spine:

Project Leviathan—Phase 3: Implantation of RFID chips in the gills of bluefin tuna.

The sea was nothing more than a giant dashboard now.

The Chamber of Echoes

Dusk bathed City Hall in a sickly phosphene glow. Evan Grey, the mayor and industrial magnate, made digital octopuses dance in a holographic aquarium. “The ocean is a spreadsheet to be optimized,” he declared, adjusting his synthetic nacre bow tie.

David slammed the hydrocarbon analysis reports onto the touchscreen. The numbers swirled before forming a map of cursed currents. “Your algorithms ignore the song of the tides,” he retorted, activating an underwater recording. The low frequencies rattled the windows—it was the voice of right whales, distorted by military sonar.

Suddenly, a digital octopus escaped the aquarium. Its pixelated tentacles traced a musical staff on the wall, the notes forming the path of clandestine pipelines. Evan Grey paled. His smartwatch beeped an alarm—140 beats per minute, the rhythm of panic.

Abyssal Nocturne

Night unfurled its shroud of black algae, swallowing the last shreds of decency. David followed the spiral-patterned pebbles into the cave, its walls covered in fluorescent petroglyphs. Clara's charred notebook lay among shattered amphorae, its surviving pages describing:

– The dance of the tides as a cryptographic key—each ebb, a password

– The alchemy of sediments transforming mercury into liquid strychnine

– The equation of current-driven evidence: √(lies) × (silence) = truth

Suddenly, the ctenophores illuminated in unison. Their cold light cast the layered shadows of the guilty on the walls: three hooded figures handling giant test tubes. The cephalopod mask split open with a shell-like creak, revealing a USB key sculpted from a narwhal's tooth. Data burst forth in luminous bubbles—each sphere containing a compromising file.

The Awakening of the Candle-Jellyfish

The assault was an underwater symphony. David raised the mask radiating hadal light, transforming the storage tanks into liquid stained-glass windows. The culprits emerged from the foam like cursed figureheads:

Dr. Silenus, his eyelids tattooed with forbidden chemical formulas

Jake Morrow, a belt studded with whale shark teeth stolen from stranded corpses

Esther Blackwood, pupils dilated from psychotropics and falsified numbers

The kite-jellyfish ascended in a geodesic swarm, their stinging filaments linked to underwater projectors. Across the flanks of the barges, the beams traced damning graphs: skyrocketing pollution curves, toxin dispersion maps, and photos of mutilated organs.

"You forgot that the sea remembers everything," David roared, activating the sound diffusion system. Clara's recordings echoed, her voice amplified by the underwater caves: Methanol weeps in C minor—listen to the sobs beneath the valves!

Epilogue: The Nereids' Hymn

David collapsed at the foot of Race Point's lighthouse, his body a reef of truths. The narwhal tooth gleamed in his open palm—a marine clepsydra marking the hour of judgment. Somewhere in the depths, Grey Marine's encrypted servers imploded under abyssal pressure, releasing torrents of data rising to the surface like confession bubbles.

Offshore, the ghost barges continued their macabre ballet, sirens wailing a chemical credo. The first schools of genetically modified mackerel had already arrived, their eyes equipped with cameras recording every move. Once again, the ocean sang its immutable hymn—a concert of creaking carcasses and lamenting waves, a requiem of living beings and lost souls. Somewhere in the chaos, a moon jellyfish pulsed gently, already writing the next chapter.

Chapter III: Compendium

The investigation leads to Grey Marine being guilty of toxic pollution. David confronts Dr. Silenus and his accomplices, dismantles a waste trafficking network, and realizes Clara was murdered for uncovering their crimes. The mutant jellyfish carry proof of contamination.

Chapter IV
The Rumors of Light-Pond

I. Trembling Dawn

Day slipped into the room through narrow gaps, unraveling the darkness into wisps of golden gauze. David Sinclair extracted himself from bed, limb by limb, like freeing oneself from a fishing net. The air carried the scent of rust and white algae—the fragrance of forgotten wrecks. On the dresser, a fossilized sea urchin used as a paperweight seemed to watch him with its thousand petrified eyes. Each opening in the mineral creature held the memory of a century of tides, shipwrecks, and dissolved secrets.

Clara's desk awaited him—a crypt of text where constellations of yellowed sticky notes lay scattered. As he opened the top drawer, his fingers brushed against a cartography of scars:

- A gannet's feather dipped in sepia ink, its quill engraved with coordinates in Morse code.
- X-rays of seashells afflicted by melanoma, their calcified spirals warped into silent screams.
- A notebook stitched with steel threads, titled Necrology of the Tides, its cover oozing amber resin with the scent of marine myrrh.

The first page exhaled a sigh of spores. Clara described "spectral tides" gnawing at the coasts during the equinox, carrying away fragments of reality. "On March 21st, at 3:17 AM, I saw the

MacMillan lighthouse vanish into a fold of mist. It still existed in the song of the hollow oysters, their shells murmuring its position at 47° 23′ N, 70° 12′ W." Below, a trembling marginal note read: "The mask is not an artifact but a serrated key. Its grooves match the meanders of our liquid memory."

David held the fossilized feather under his UV lamp. The barbs glowed, revealing verses in Old Breton etched into the keratin:

"Ken a vo mor, a vo koun"

(As long as there is the sea, there will be memory.)

II. The Old Man and the Cenotaph

Isaac waited in front of his "wreckage museum"—a shack of planks where the ghosts of the bay had taken refuge. Shattered bows exhaled their agony; delirious sextants pointed toward vanished stars. The old sailor stroked a buoy from Lady Margaret, a ship that disappeared in 1923 with twelve souls and a cargo of mercury. "She came here every full moon," he murmured, running his fingers over an octopus-shaped barometer. Its dial still read 1034 hPa—the exact pressure of the night the ship sank.

When he cranked up the worn phonograph, the needle carved a groove into the wax, releasing a distorted siren's melody. The dusty windowpanes vibrated in unison. "That's the Calliope of the Abyss... She guides souls to the coral cities," Isaac explained, pointing to a mummified sunfish floating in a jar.

In its quartz-like pupils, David thought he saw Clara's reflection—her mouth open on a secret too vast for a human body, her hair transformed into bioluminescent algae.
"And that?" David pointed to a compass locked inside a glass sphere filled with black water.
"The magnetic heart of the pelican. It still points north… from 90 years ago."

III. The Equinox Café

The café smelled of cinnamon and absinthe, an acrid blend sailors called "siren's breath." Behind the counter, a percolator groaned like a ship's boiler, expelling steam in the shape of a jellyfish. The waitress—constellations tattooed beneath her collarbone—set an espresso before David. Her bluish nails left flecks of polish on the saucer.
"Clara always ordered The Wrecker—a triple espresso drowned in Virgin Islands rum."
A fisherman, his beard embedded with mica flakes, leaned in, his breath thick with fermented kelp. "I saw her talking to a school of herring. They swam in spirals around her… Like a Morse prayer." His calloused hands mimicked aquatic swirls.
David noted every detail in his notebook, its pages absorbing lies and fractured truths like blotting paper. On page 34, a sketch of Clara appeared—drawings of lanternfish forming a luminous alphabet.

IV. The Bookstore with Silk Eyelids

The sign read Maelström, concealing a labyrinth of driftwood carvings. The bookseller—her eyes rimmed in midnight-blue kohl—stroked an ancient book bound in stingray leather, leaving phosphorescent trails on its cover.

"Clara was looking for this."

She handed him a volume titled Litanies of Davy Jones' Brides. The pages released a cloud of starfish dust, momentarily forming the constellation of Scorpio.

"These women wed the currents to become guardians of the straits. Their songs make reefs sprout from shipwrecked corpses."

In the margin, a trembling annotation in red ink read:

"The mask is their cursed dowry—an interface between breaths."

David felt a deep vibration in his legs as if the ocean beneath him whispered millennia-old equations into his bones.

V. The Embrace of the Sargasso

Lila stood barefoot on the beach, her feet sinking into the icy sand. Around her, electric-blue jellyfish washed ashore in silence, their bells pulsing like freshly removed hearts.

“They know you’re coming,” she murmured, pointing to the horizon where a mirage of underwater spires floated. “Last night, the fiddler crabs migrated east… Their claws scraped the sand in a pavane rhythm. A sign that the Guardians are restless.”

She handed him a vial containing a lantern shark embryo.

“Clara called this her ‘pocket lighthouse.’ When its bioluminescence activates…”

The tiny creature glowed, projecting shifting hieroglyphs onto the sand, recomposing themselves with each wave.

David read two words, repeated in echo:

"Dive."

"Forget."

VI. The Sway of Algae Pendulums

In his room, David laid out the evidence on the bed:

1. The notebook with serpentine phrases, its pages breathing to the rhythm of the tides.
2. Isaac's cryptic recording, whose low frequencies matched the pulses of the Humboldt Current.
3. The blinking lantern shark, its belly now revealing diving diagrams.

The floor vibrated to the rhythm of the waves. Shadows lengthened, taking humanoid shapes with crustacean-like joints. A voice slipped into his left ear, warm and briny:

"All truth is a voluntary shipwreck. Release your breath; let the abyss write you."

He opened the notebook to a page marked by an ink stain shaped like a lost continent. Clara described a ritual of "inverted baptism," where initiates drank the ocean until their lungs became aquariums populated by symbiotic chimeras.

When the lantern shark flickered off, only one certainty remained:

Tomorrow, he would face the deep.

Somewhere in the night, a sonar buoy emitted three spaced beeps—a message in Gray code that only a man on borrowed time could decipher.

Epilogue

At dawn, David stood on the pier, gazing at the phantom reefs of Stellwagen Bank. In his pocket, the embryonic shark pulsed faintly—a biological compass leading to the underwater labyrinths.

Above him, gulls traced a word in the sky that he recognized:

"Dive."

And the ocean, always the ocean, stretched its foamy arms toward him.

Chapter IV: Compendium

David delves into local myths and sailor rituals. According to the records, Clara studied the Brides of Davy Jones—women transformed into marine guardians. The mask, a key to the abyss, guides David toward underwater caves where Clara left cryptic clues.

Chapter V
The Liturgies of Sediment

I. The Dawn of Gills

Day pierced the horizon, tearing open a pocket of night, spilling an opiate light over Provincetown. David Sinclair emerged from his room; his skin streaked with dreams where calligrapher octopuses inscribed enigmas across his torso. The epidermal patterns still pulsed, each ink-darkened suction mark corresponding to an abyssal pressure point. The air smelled of oxidized zinc and plastic bags transfigured into jellyfish—a scent of a dying century clinging to the mucous membranes like a saline cobweb.

The municipal library lay dormant, a neo-Gothic structure whose windows were veiled in dried seaweed. As David pushed the door open, he stepped into a lung of paper, where memory-laden spores drifted through the air. The bookshelves quivered softly, their warped planks breathing the exhalations of forbidden tomes. Between two incunabula, translucent sea cucumbers filtered the particles of lost knowledge.

The curator—her eyes rimmed with abyssal kohl—emerged from a cloud of starfish dust. Her stingray silk-gloved fingers handed him The Geographies of Marine Disaster, bound with still-quivering squid tendons.

"The Borealis did not sink, Lieutenant. It disincarnated," she whispered, caressing a medallion of amber where a remora larva twirled endlessly. The pages bled in her hands, revealing maps of cursed currents drawn in tubeworm blood.

"Look here." Her iridescent fingernail pointed to a vortex off Georges Bank. "The tides there dance in counterpoint to tectonic mazurkas. Clara heard the faults singing…"

II. The Choir of Floating Scars

At the harbor, trawlers choreographed a disjointed pavane to the sound of sonar buoys pulsing in liquid Morse code. David questioned Jethro, a fisherman whose face was overtaken by symbiotic coral, his gnarled hands carving lures from dentures scavenging along the shore.

"The Borealis?" The man spat a jet of black tobacco juice that burned a hole into the rotted wood. "My great-grandfather said it sails between raindrops. On stormy nights, you can see its mist-lace sails catching the moonbeams."

Around them, the crews nodded, brandishing hooks braided with the hair of drowned men. Pete, the bosun with plankton-injected eyes, displayed a femur polished by the tides: "Clara came to measure our scars. She said they were like underwater fissures—each scratch a deep ravine, each burn an explosion of methane gas."

David noted their words in a waterproof notebook, the ink dissolving into blue tendrils upon contact with the ambient salt. On page 67, a jellyfish-cartographer emerged spontaneously, its filaments tracing the coordinates 42° 58′ N, 67° 57′ W.

III. The Scriptorium of Osmotic Shadows

Clara's office had transformed into a marine sorcery lab. Among the waterproof binders, miniature aquariums housed diatoms arranged into shimmering sentences. David deciphered their flickering message:

"The mask is an airlock—cross it only with new gills."

The final syllable burst in a spray of green bioluminescence, projecting the shadow of a giant squid onto the ceiling, its suction cups inscribed with scripture. In the secret drawer behind the herbarium of dead skin, he found slivers of swimmers' epidermis marked with bioluminescent tattoos. Clara had annotated:

"Day 7: The capillaries become algae—photosynthesis of despair."

A whale-wax-sealed envelope contained photographs of a humanoid shadow with crustacean-jointed limbs, its webbed hand reaching toward the lens in silent supplication.

On the back, her fevered handwriting:

"They know we are plundering their nacreous library. The abyssal shelves groan under tomes of chitin..."

IV. The Crypt of Gelatinous Bells

The lighthouse swayed gently, a hypnotic pendulum, its beam extinguished since the night of the Great Cataclysm. In the lantern room, repurposed into an excavation studio, jars of cryogenized jellyfish pulsed as David approached. Among vials of synthetic mermaid tears, the mask lay upon a cushion of fossilized skate eggs—each capsule containing a grotesque embryo of truth.

The artifact vibrated in harmony with the tides, its hollow eye sockets exuding a violet mist that sketched fractal patterns of hidden currents in the air. As he lifted it, David felt his fingerprints shift—his epidermal ridges morphing into freshwater channels, liquid labyrinths leading to forgotten arteries.

A chitinous creak.

Richard appeared—unrecognizable. His skin had sprouted marine taste buds; his slit-pupiled eyes glowed with an alien intelligence.

"She forced the floodgates," he gurgled, brandishing a narwhal-tooth scalpel streaked with psychotropic venom. "Now the archivists have come to reclaim their books of flesh."

V. The Procession of Chlorophyll-Flayed Beings

The confrontation erupted into a frenzied chase across the dunes of flavor. Richard—now a Marine God—projected jets of blue amino acid, transmuting the sand into toxic lace. The mask adhered to David's face, his lungs splitting into aerial sacs—an amphibian adaptation accompanied by the taste of rust and seaweed.

In their wake, the dunes birthed skeletons of ghost ships. Translucent crews chanted tide tables in Old Norse, their voices synchronized with the crackle of beached crystal radios.

Clara appeared—now a sentient mass of aggregated zooplankton—and traced a warm-water current circle in the air:

"The Borealis was a mere decoy. Seek the Geosynclinal Cephalopod—it has been weaving continents since the Cretaceous. Its inks flow through the veins of the tectonic plates..."

VI. The Apotheosis of Opposable Inks

The town hall had transformed into an abyssal cathedral. Evan Grey sat enthroned within an exoskeleton of black coral, his limbs manipulated by lever-pulled octopuses. "We are the scribes of the Great Mucus," he boomed, projecting holograms of sunken cities where figures with moonfish eyes stirred. "Clara broke the pact of sedimentary silence. Now the abyss demands its due."

David brandished the mask—now organic—its edges covered in vibrating cilia emitting a purifying ultrasonic tone. The object unleashed the cry of a fossilized whale, fracturing the walls and revealing the ocean beneath: book-creatures with membranous pages swam through the rifts, devouring paragraphs of corrupted reality.

Clara merged with the Geosynclinal Cephalopod, her encyclopedia-tentacles rewriting marine DNA in real-time.

"Your time will come," she murmured, erasing Evan Grey letter by letter, each consonant falling away like a charred scale.

"The abyssal librarians await you for the Great Cataloging…"

Epilogue: The Symbiosis

David awoke on the shore, the mask now fused to his face in perfect symbiosis. His new variable-focus eyes discerned limestone cities beneath the sand—living architectures where the shadows of redeemed drowned souls moved.

Within him, Clara whispered poems in lost languages, each verse tinting the flow of his altered hemocyanins.

The sea lapped knowingly.

Somewhere in the deep, the colossal squid's giant quill traced their story into the Book of Sediments, a vast grimoire where every grain of sand was a comma in the oceanic epic.

Chapter V: Compendium

Hunted by Evan Grey's henchmen, David uses the mask to communicate with marine creatures. He discovers an underwater laboratory where humans have been hybridized with abyssal fauna. Clara, now a bioluminescent entity, reveals to him that the ocean is a living archive.

Chapter VI
The Liturgies of the Abyss

I. Morning of Venom and Vellum

Dawn licked Provincetown with a tongue of mercury, revealing rooftops curved like overturned hulls. David Sinclair walked on the glistening cobblestones, each step awakening mosaics of shells trapped in cement. These limestone tesserae formed a silent alphabet—forgotten runes of tides that had once eroded the boundaries between land and sea. The night before, he had dreamed of Clara carving prayers into the shell of a fiddler crab, her scissors releasing a pungent scent of burnt plankton that still lingered on his fingers.

The library lay dormant, like a stone sphinx whose eyes were panes of glass tinted by algae. The curator—her hair woven with diatom filaments—opened the grimoire Necrology of the Tides, bound in dried squid tendons that still pulsed faintly. The pages exhaled a cloud of cuttlebone dust as the title bled in phosphorescent letters: "The dead also write in the gaps of low tide."

David discovered schematics of ghost ships digested by the Gulf Stream, their frames transformed into sentient reefs. In the margins, Clara's handwriting trembled like a seismic line: "Shipwreck is metamorphosis: the crew becomes an ecosystem, and their cries turn into bubbles in the songs of whales."

II. The Choir of Speaking Scars

At the port, trawlers snapped their moorings in liquid Morse code. A fisherman, his face devoured by barnacles, displayed a mummified hand whose gnarled fingers bore tattoos of abyssal constellations. "It still catches on nights of the new moon," he growled, twirling the desiccated appendage. "The Borealis' cook lost it while slicing a giant squid—his final recipe."
Around them, sailors lined up vials of marine humor:

- Electric jellyfish sweat pulsing to an underwater tango rhythm
- Crystallized humpback whale tears, refracting melancholic light
- A blown-glass inkwell filled with the sepia of a sepulchral octopus

"Clara came to sample our old wounds," muttered an old man, lifting his flesh-knit sweater to reveal scars left by rope burns. His marks traced the exact path of clandestine pipelines. David felt his own scars pulse in response—saltwater burns rising from the depths of his memory.

III. The Sepulcher of Osmotic Writings

The lighthouse groaned with rotting wood as David entered the necromarine laboratory. The air was thick with phrases cut from logbooks, swimming in shoals of words within aquariums of liquid oxygen. A tide clock—made of fossilized shark teeth—ticked in reverse, each click synchronized with the heartbeat of a drowned soul.

Behind a curtain of freeze-dried seaweed, the mask lay on a bed of desiccated gills. Its eye sockets, now filled with blinking bioluminescent jelly, flickered in Hadal code. Lifting it, David felt his fingerprints bud into suction cups—the mutation reaching its climax. The mask began to sing, blending the voice of a sperm whale with Clara's intonations: "You shall be the wandering encyclopedia of our lost ones, each suction cup a page, each tentacle an index."

IV. The Dance of the Flayed Chlorophyll

The final confrontation took place in the town hall, transformed into an underwater cathedral. Evan Grey sat enthroned within an exoskeleton of black coral, mechanical octopuses maneuvering his limbs, entangled in bureaucratic pseudopods. Behind him, an aquarium housed clones of Clara in controlled decay—beta versions with atrophied gills.

"The Borealis is a process," he sneered, projecting holograms of investors fused with moray eels. The digital creatures wove a saraband around cursed pipeline blueprints. "We don't trade in oil, Sinclair, but in fossilized memories—each gallon is the sigh of a prehistoric sea creature."

David brandished the mask, now pulsing as living flesh. Clara's duplicates pressed against the glass, whispering in unison: "We are the archivists of oblivion—the guardians of thresholds where ships become legends."

V. The Call of the Geosynclinal Cephalopod

David fled to the caves where Clara had traced her final equations. The ceiling wept limestone tears forming musical staves—echoes of toxic symphonies. Fossilized octopuses on the walls mapped out forbidden currents, their dried inks mirroring the striations of the mask. The artifact came to life in a crackle of abyssal bubbles. Its amber tentacles pierced David's eardrums, tearing the veil of perception.

Visions:

- The Borealis sailing through layers of time, its hull gnawed by prophetic anemones
- The crew transformed into a sentient reef, their brains replaced by nautilus minds.
- Clara swimming among them, her pulsating gills fanned in a chromatic spectrum

"The wreck is a gateway," roared a voice composed of billions of diatoms. "The dead demand royalties over the living—payable in breath and salt."

VI. The Ordination of Abyssal Scribes

The ship graveyard revealed the Borealis lying in its shroud of black sand. Humanoid shadows with lighthouse-lens eyes emerged from its ruptured hull, chanting tide tables in Old Norse. Clara appeared, her body woven from strands of marine DNA and fluorescent microplastics—the ultimate synthesis of her research.

"The true treasure was never on board," she intoned, pointing to the seabed. David dug. His flesh-turned-dredging-tools unearthed a library of whale skulls—each bone engraved with collective memories in Hadal script. The mask exploded in a rain of diatoms that embedded into his skin, inscribing their shared history in phosphorescent letters.

Epilogue: The Baptism of Opposable Inks

David awoke on the shore, his body converted into a living grimoire. His tattoos narrated the story of the Borealis in serpentine phrases, each comma a drop of modified hemocyanin. The lighthouse flickered in marine Morse: "Welcome among the scribes of the deep—your ink will flow with the great currents."

Somewhere beneath his feet, Clara and the crew continued writing the ghost ship's epic. Their quills—carved from fossilized shark teeth—scratched the ocean floor, composing an infinite symphony for a choir of jellyfish and an orchestra of tides.

The sea finally smiled, reclaiming its ternary rhythm: breath, tide, rebirth.

Chapter VI: Compendium

A storm forces David to ally with rebel fishermen. Together, they sabotage clandestine pipelines. Clara appears in a vision, explaining that the lost ones are "reef sowers" sacrificed to regenerate the ecosystem. Evan Grey drowns, devoured by a creature from the depths.

Chapter VII
The Liturgies of the Sclerochronologist

I. The Dawn of Palimpsest Striations

The sun dissected the horizon into stratigraphic cross-sections, irradiating Provincetown with a faceted light. David advanced between the hydrophobic markers; each step awakening echoes of forgotten basalts. The rocks sang in ultra-infrasound, prehistoric oratorios compressed from the voices of the primordial oceans. The air was thick with the scent of bioluminescent lichen and marine rust—an acrid blend that clung to the gums like an aborted confession.

In the bunker lined with bathymetric maps, Evan Grey calibrated glacial cores streaked with the scars of commercial wars.

"We don't archive time, Sinclair. We torment it."

His chitinous gloves extracted a sedimentary disk: 1812, 1944, 2023… Concentric layers trapping the effluvia of programmed shipwrecks. A scanner detected nanoparticles of shattered portholes embedded in limestone—fragments of vitrified memory.

II. The Sanctuary of the Symbiotes

The New Library undulated on a bed of mutant seagrasses, its walls of cyanobacterial vesicles pulsing in sync with the toxic tides. The curator—her thorax fused with a giant ascidian—presented codices copied by polyglot annelids.

"Observe," she murmured, opening a manuscript on jellyfish skin, "our scribes digest the chronicles. Their cloacae birth parchments of abyssal cellulose."

David consulted the Otolith of the Dead Tides, its growth rings illuminated by biophores. A pulsating line revealed:

"The Borealis incubated Siboglinids. Their plumes contain the necrotic manifesto."

In a hyperbaric chamber, Clara communed with a tube worm, her vibratile cilia modulating semantic waves. Holograms of deceased captains danced around her, spectral echoes encoded in mitochondrial DNA.

III. The Ordeal of the Growth Rings

The quay, transformed into an alchemical laboratory, fumed with sediment crucibles. Fishermen underwent paradoxical transfigurations under the vacant gaze of Arctic terns:

- The Deckhand: Arms grafted with coelacanth fins, skin infused with mnemonic phytoplankton.
- The Sailor's Wife: Estuarine varices distilling a gin scented with shipwrecks, each sip exposing a fragment of a sunken logbook.
- The Dockworker: Sternum pierced with stalactites of rock salt, crystals vibrating at hadal frequencies, chanting litanies of lost cargoes.

"Clara was deciphering our medullary rings," explained a man whose vertebrae were striated like mangrove trunks. Lifting his shirt, he revealed growth rings mapping the routes of the Borealis.

"Our bones recount the transgressions of the currents."

IV. The Repository of Annals

The inverted lighthouse—a limestone column buried beneath three centuries of compressed shells—housed an abyssal scriptorium. Cephalopodic robots calligraphed on mesoglea scrolls, their inks composed of archaic pheromones and synthetic siren tears. The air smelled of ozone and rotten vanilla—the perfume of buried truths.

The mask lay in a chamber of siliceous resonance, its eye sockets colonized by diatom-clavicles emitting signals in fossil Morse code. When David made contact, he felt his neural connections reorganizing into prehistoric fractal patterns, as if his consciousness were merging with the cycles of the world. Images of undulating tectonic plates flooded his mind, a telluric ballet orchestrated by the wingbeats of prehistoric pteropods.

"It breathes," articulated a voice from the rocky substratum.

Evan Grey emerged, clad in a suit that disintegrated into a network of legal regulations and bylaws.

"We did not forge it. We fertilized it. Every shipwreck is fertilizer."

V. The March of the Chronovores

The encounter culminated in a vertiginous plunge down the escarpments of Lophelia Pertusa, where masses of black algae buzzed with temporal creatures. Grey climbed a wall covered in palimpsest glyphs, his limbs extending into administrative stolons.

"The Borealis is an organ!" he roared as contractual clauses sprouted from his sleeves. Hybridized real estate developers, fused with electronic moray eels, slithered from the crevices, wielding notarized deeds engraved on narwhal teeth.

David brandished the mask, now a quantum amplifier. Clara's clones chanted a counterpoint litany of the tides, triggering a telluric resonance. The ground cracked open, revealing the true Borealis—a vessel of cartilage and silica, its masts bristling with prophetic hydroids. Fossilized crews continued engraving tablets of petrified ivory, their chisels carving furrows into time itself.

Clara appeared, her hair now composed of thylakoid membranes pulsing to the rhythm of solar tides.

"They record the song of the ridges," she whispered, caressing a pebble marked with the Ordovician seal.

"Since the Archean era, every tsunami has been a stanza."

VI. The Intronization of the Scribes

In the crypts of the vessel-organism, David discovered the ultimate archive—kilometers of galleries populated by ctenophore-books emitting bioluminescent signals. The shelves, made of genetically modified trilobite carapaces, held chitin scrolls engraved with the memory of typhoons.

The mask fused to his skin, its suction cups linking his limbic system to the global trophic network. An exquisite pain radiated through his ribcage as his bones metamorphosed into nautilus clavicles.

"Welcome, dear journalists!" exclaimed Clara, now a collective of sentient radiolarians. She pointed to a chimera-membrane scroll where their names shimmered in hadal script.

"Begin your stanza. Write with the blood of the tides."

Evan Grey collapsed into a pit of anoxic brine, his final words fossilizing into methane hydrates. David felt his memories seep away through the ostioles, replaced by the recollections of proto-plankton—a vertiginous experience where each diatom became a chapter.

Epilogue: The Tectonic Glyphs

David awoke on the shore, his body transformed into a living stele. His tattoos narrated the epic of the Borealis in piezophilic hieroglyphs, each symbol exalting with the movements of subcutaneous currents. The lighthouse flickered in bioluminescent code:
"Write the next tide.
Your ink is the blood of the abyss."
Beneath the sands, Clara and the ghostly crew engraved new stanzas into the oceanic plates. Their chisels, fashioned from fossilized shark teeth, carved grooves into the Earth's mantle—each line a potential earthquake.
The mask, grafted to his sternum, modulated the hymn of the hadal chroniclers—a melody of bubbles and polar ice creaks. The ocean breathed, its abysses turning the pages of the world's telluric grimoire, already preparing the next cataclysmic epilogue.

Chapter VII: Compendium

David investigates an opioid trafficking operation concealed within shipments of salt. He meets Anaïs, a child witness to illegal experiments, and discovers that Clara had been protecting victims of a pedo-criminal network. Isaac, an old sailor, sacrifices himself to save them during an ambush.

Chapter VIII
The Tidewriter

I. The Hour of the Gray Nuptials

Provincetown awoke in an inverted twilight, the mist giving birth to a pale day where the contours of reality blurred. Beached boats seemed to float inches above the ground, their leprous hulls oozing a resin of melancholy. David Sinclair followed a trail of shattered clams, each containing a fragment of broken mirror reflecting an absent sky.

Sheriff McAllister's office occupied the former cabin of the Lady's Sorrow, a three-masted ship converted into a floating prison a century earlier. The oak walls buckled under the assault of invisible shipworms.

"Your ghosts have the tenacity of barnacles, Sinclair," the sheriff growled, tapping a sea chart riddled with wormholes. "They cling to the bellies of wrecks and devour the wood down to the sapwood of memories."

Inside the cells, infused with specters, three figures draped in sailcloth shrouds spoke in the tongue of countercurrents. Their frayed fingers wove nets of mist where drowned syllables became entangled.

David placed a block of peat, streaked with cryptic markings, on the desk. "Clara carved her testament into the salt marsh peat. These incisions..." He traced a perfect spiral.

It was the last breath, trapped between the tides of the sea.

A beam of light pierced through the rotting planks, suddenly illuminating the glyphs. They flickered to the rhythm of a forgotten heartbeat.

II. The Scriptorium of Liquid Shadows

The old cannery exhaled a sigh of rust as they pushed open the door. Hundreds of jars lined decayed shelves, containing parchment-like jellyfish, their forms swaying in a silent rhythm against walls covered in calligraphed algae.

Lila awaited them near a vat of living ink. Dressed in a gown woven from scraps of fishing nets, she herself seemed to hover inches above the ground.

"She conversed with the drowned from the deep," she murmured, handing him a scroll made of stingray membrane. "Their letters rise through hydrothermal vents, carried by submarine winds."

The spiraling script shimmered with a bioluminescent glow. David read fragments of a diary interwoven with deranged oceanographic notes:

"5:32 AM. The floor sings in F-sharp minor. The corals write sonnets in the sand. I have become the semicolon between two waves."

Suddenly, the jars trembled. The jellyfish traced syncopated stanzas of cold light, projecting onto the walls the spectral ballet of the lost souls of Borealis. Clara stood at the center, her translucent body encircled by creatures with shadowy tentacles.

III. The Song of the Faults

Evan Grey presided over a cavern hollowed into the foundations of the abandoned lighthouse. Machines bristling with seismic probes moaned softly, their screens displaying blue lava rivers snaking beneath the earth's crust.

"They seek the primordial fault," he growled, brandishing a stylus carved from a cetacean bone. "The scar where the lies of continents are swallowed. The Borealis was just bait for something bigger."

He stabbed the tool into a table covered in demonic sea charts. The ground trembled, unleashing a rumble that sent salt stalactites spinning. Vials filled with abyssal sediments erupted into a dissonant chorus—the notes aligned with a long-forgotten earthquake.

"Her body..." David began, his throat tight with the stench of sulfur.

Grey pushed aside a curtain of rusted chains, revealing a basin where a dark reflection swam, its hair woven with electric seaweed.

"She has become ink in the book of the abyss. Her blood flows through the veins of the Gulf Stream; her bones are the characters of an alphabet that defies the tides."

The creature raised a diaphanous hand. On its surface, words in marine Morse code emerged, traced by bioluminescent parasites:

"Do not seek—listen. The wrecks are commas in the story of the waves."

The Office of the Low Tides

The final scene unfolded on a black shale beach streaked with bloody quartz. Children, their eyes pale as sea foam, built a lighthouse from the charred bones of the Borealis. Isaac, his face weathered by tempests of lies, handed David an inkwell fashioned from a giant sea urchin.

"She lives in the margins now," he said, pointing to the horizon where a ghost ship drifted. "Between the word and the silence, in the blank space that separates twin waves."

The flask contained a shifting ink where mermaid scales floated. David dipped a driftwood stylus into it. As it touched the sand, the first drop traced a perfect word: epilogue.

Suddenly, the entire bay held its breath. The waves froze in crests of frosted glass. Across the wet sand, entire phrases appeared—Clara's testament, written in the alphabet of the ocean depths.

"The drowned do not die. They stretch beneath the kelp, vertebral columns of a poem that the sea rewrites with every tide. Seek me in the whisper of shells, in the groan of overstrained moorings. I am the fermata between two tides, the sigh that separates the wave from the foam."

As the sun finally pierced the clouds, David found an intact notebook at his feet. Its pages, covered in familiar handwriting, all began with the same phrase:

"This is not an ending, but a maelstrom…"

Epilogue: The Abyss Watcher

That night, the fishermen reported a strange occurrence: the abandoned lighthouse had relit itself, projecting not a beam of light but entire phrases onto the waves. Every hour, a new stanza emerged from its lantern, written in a fire that burned salt without the veil of night.

Watching from the cliff, David knew he would never publish the article. The truth belonged to the tides now. Instead, he whispered into the ear of the wind:

"Write well, Clara. Write for all the silences that never found a shore."

Somewhere in the depths, a giant squid consumed its ink and began anew.

Chapter VIII: Compendium

Senator Callahan, mastermind of the trafficking operation, is unmasked. David and Lila, a journalist, infiltrate a warehouse where children are being held. Anaïs, possessing marine knowledge inherited from her father, activates a sound signal that detonates bombs hidden beneath orphanages.

Chapter IX
The Metamorphoses of Low Tide

I. The Hour of Soluble Marks

The sea had made Clara different. Her body lay on the shore, wrapped in a tunic of dried foam, her hair braided with nocturnal seaweed. David was unsurprised to see that the markings had changed: the bluish spirals on her nape had unfurled into floral arabesques as if death were continuing its work in invisible ink.

"She has become a bridge," explained the old taxidermist assigned to perform the autopsy. His hands, scarred with scalpel marks, pointed to the palms of the deceased. "Look at these striations. Milky Ways of new skin."

David wrote "metamorphosis" in capital letters in his notebook, underlining it three times. The same word had appeared in the report of the 1947 shipwreck survivor—the one whose heart had grown coral roots.

Beyond the fog, the lighthouse suddenly flashed a brief, long, brief signal. **Alert.**

II. The Theater of Skins

The abandoned cannery exuded a smell of kelp and repressed confessions. Lila awaited them near vats where jellyfish-scrolls floated, their undulating forms casting liquid stanzas onto the walls.

"You're looking for a monster, but the real crime is under your eyelids," she said, unrolling a strip of sharkskin tattooed with numbers. "She shed her flesh like an old dress. Now, she inhabits the tides."

David touched the damp wall. Beneath his fingers, the concrete trembled faintly. Muffled voices recited the wreck of the Borealis in an endless loop—not the documented crash, but a slow, voluptuous submersion, like a sheet being pulled over a lover.

In a forgotten jar, squid larvae had traced a word as they danced: **flayed**.

III. The Confession of the Cliffs

Sheriff McAllister had converted his office into a morbid cabinet of curiosities. Between an orca skull and storm bottles, he turned a rusted key before the flame of an oil lamp.

"Grey collects skins," he muttered without preamble. "Not furs—epidermises. Those who disappear... leave behind an empty shell in the sea caves."

He opened a chest of black wood. Inside were twelve rolls of human parchment tattooed with family constellations. David recognized Clara's nape—her spirals now frozen into a cartography of cursed straits.

"The mask is just a decoy," the sheriff continued, caressing a fragment of the sculpted vertebra. "What they're after is the core. The bone beneath the bone. The word before the tongue."

A gust of wind extinguished the lamp. When the light returned, the chest was empty.

IV. The Office of the Living Flayed

The final scene unfolded in the underwater chapel, accessible only at low tide. David moved between barnacle-covered pillars, his torch illuminating niches where figures trembled, wrapped in a nacreous membrane.

Grey awaited him before the basalt altar, clad in a chasuble made of a thousand ray scales.

"You don't see clearly, Sinclair. These bodies aren't corpses—they're chrysalides."

He pulled on a chain. The ground shuddered, releasing a geyser of sand filled with bioluminescent particles. One by one, the membranes tore open, revealing adolescents with eyes like empty seas.

Clara emerged from the darkness, adorned in a new form, a mask of living cartilage. "The real crime is being born into a single skin," she intoned as the water began to rise.

David felt his scars reopen in perfect spirals.

Epilogue: The Blood of the Tides

At dawn, fishermen found David's notebook washed up in a bed of kelp.

The last pages, gnawed by saltwater, contained only one readable sentence:

"We are all flayed beings, dancing on the graves of our former skins."

The lighthouse now flashes in cycles of twelve beats. On nights of high tide, the cliffs seem to hum—a chorus of childlike voices chanting the alphabet of metamorphoses.

Chapter IX: Compendium

Anaïs guides David to a trapped submarine. They disable bombs rigged to the tides while Isaac, returned in spectral form, disrupts enemy systems. Clara, fused with plankton, releases a toxin that neutralizes the criminals.

Chapter X
The Ink Masters of Absence

I. The Hour of Phantom Inks

The bookstore Aux Mots Perdus exuded a scent of fish glue and ancient regrets. David Sinclair pushed aside the sticky cobwebs blocking the entrance, his fingers brushing against sharkskin-bound books. The moon filtered through the dusty windows, iridescent on the open pages scattered across the floor like fallen blades.

The corpse lay curled in a fetal position before a copy of The Abyssal Chronicles. The man—his fifties worn thin by rum and bad choices—seemed to have bled from every pore. The coroner, a freckled Scotsman, lifted a kerosene lamp:

"Look at this." The flickering light revealed words carved into the flesh of the forearms. I have another one on the right. Ink always flows toward the abyss on the left.

David jotted down the inscriptions in his grease-stained notebook, the same sharp focus he had used on the anonymous letters sent to Clara. In the dead man's pocket, a cigar case held three human teeth and a scrap of parchment inscribed: Kemp lives in the margins.

Suddenly, the scratch of a quill on the vellum. On the second floor, a shadow in a bowler hat feverishly copied Moby Dick onto a roll of human parchment. David drew his Webley, but by the time he reached the mezzanine, all that remained was a still-warm whale-tooth pen.

II. The Scriptorium of Shadowed Letters

The underground printing press reeked of molten lead and the sweat of overworked machines. Mabel Whitby, 87 years old with owl-like eyes, adjusted her pince-nez before a stone slab covered in sea-runes.

"Kemp wrote with giant squid ink. His words... moved beneath the page."

She pointed to a trapdoor hidden under rolls of Bible paper. In the flooded basement, David found twelve watertight crates. The first contained The Sermons of the Mad Tides by Clara Bishop—an uncensored edition. The marginal notes sketched a map leading to the Lighthouse of Clear Souls.

"He recycled failed writers," Mabel whispered, stroking a skull labeled Chapter XXIII: Stylistic Liquidation. "Their bones became printing type. Their screams..."

A sharp crack interrupted her. Overhead, rolls of paper unraveled, unfurling murderous phrases. David Sinclair lies about his wound in Hanover, proclaiming the dripping ink. He abandoned his sister in the fire.

The gunshot shattered the silence. Mabel collapsed, a dark stain spreading across her cheek.

In the doorway, the shadow in the bowler hat held a smoking Derringer.

III. The Interrogation of Palimpsests

Sheriff McAllister's office resembled a torture chamber for bibliophiles. Torn pages hung from butcher hooks, and every torch bore a word censored in acid.

"Grey traffics in memories," the sheriff thundered, throwing a ledger bound in whale sinew onto the desk. "He buys the debts of cursed writers. Their souls become… recurring characters."

David flipped through the register. The victims' names are intertwined with lost works. Beside Clara Bishop, a blood-red annotation: Rewriting scheduled for the equinox.

A commotion shattered the night's stillness. On Pier No. 7, a massive sheet of paper burned, spitting alphabetic embers. The swirling letters formed a testamentary phrase:

TRUE WORDS KILL LIKE THE HIGH TIDE.

In the smoldering ruins, David found a mahogany box filled with farewell letters—all written in a child's hand. The last one, dated that very day, bore a chilling postscript:

Kemp waits in the cemetery of dead phrases.

IV. The Night of the Bloodstained Editors

The crypt of Saint-Maël's Church sagged under the weight of stacked grimoires. Evan Grey adjusted his moray-skin tie before a wall of labeled skulls.

"You persist, Sinclair? Even Rimbaud knew you can't fight ghosts with conjugated verbs."

He opened a folio bound in human leather. The pages contained Clara's diary, rewritten in the third person.

"The audience loves well-crafted martyrs. Real deaths lack… style."

David retrieved the pen found on the corpse. The whale-tooth quill trembled as it touched the vellum of The Abyssal Chronicles. Lost phrases surfaced in palimpsestic layers, exposing the trade of cursed manuscripts.

Suddenly, the books came alive. Sticky vines of words wrapped around Grey as Nietzschean quotes burst from the walls.

"You see?" he growled, struggling against the parasitic paragraphs. "Even the dead plagiarize!"

V. The Dawn of Burned Pages

The lighthouse trembled under the assault of demon waves. David climbed the stairs, their steps engraved with aphorisms, his revolver loaded with Bible-etched bullets.

In the machine room—transformed into an infernal printing press—Grey manipulated a hydraulic press fed by living ink.

"Readers crave blood!" he howled, brandishing an obsidian paper-knife. "Even God rewrites his Gospels with every tide!"

David plunged his hand into a vat of voracious ink. The printing type came alive, forming a cage of lethal phrases around Grey.

"The plagiarism of the soul comes with a price," David quoted Kemp.

When the police arrived, they found Grey shackled by cushioned stanzas, his face tattooed with the first chapter of The Apocalypse According to Saint Peter. The cursed books burned silently, their ashes tracing an unprecedented constellation in the sky:

The Prosecutor of the Word.

Epilogue: The Epistolary Tides

A month later, David wandered the corridors of the abandoned library. The walls wept poisoned parables, their droplets forming micro-stories on the floor.
In the marine maps room, he found an unsent letter from Clara. The sepia ink described a phantom island where failed writers became characters. The postscript read:
"The only unforgivable crimes are the ellipses left behind as an inheritance."
On nights of strong literary winds, one can hear Grey reciting sacrilegious limericks in his cell. The jailers claim his words make toxic lichens sprout between the rocks and that prisoners consume them to compose flawless poems.
As for David, he still roams the docks, his notebook filled with unanswered questions. Sometimes, when the fog stifles the cries of seagulls, he swears he sees a shadow in a bowler hat copying his story into a book of living flesh.

Chapter X: Compendium

In the maritime library, David deciphers Clara's journal, revealing that the Watchers are humans chosen by the ocean to transcribe its memories. Evan Grey, transformed into a sea monster, is defeated through the mask.

Chapter XI
The Knots of Silence

I. The Hour of Raw Marks

The sea regurgitated its secrets at dawn's troubled light. David Sinclair leaned over the body washed up against the pier's pilings, his overcoat snapping in the wind heavy with sea spray. The corpse— a man in his thirties, his features carved by the tides— bore the same bluish spirals on his wrists as Clara. Parallel streaks ran from his palms to his elbows as if he had tried to grasp burning embers.

"Third one in fifteen days," growled Dr. Leblanc, lifting the drowned man's left eyelid. His coat, stiff with dried salt, crackled with every movement. "Same corneal edema. As if they stared at the lighthouse until blindness took them before they jumped."

David jotted down details in his angular handwriting: unmarked clothing, clean fingernails beneath recent grime, a thin rope mark around the neck. Inside the pocket of the soaked vest— a Moleskine notebook, its pages crinkled from seawater. The entries dated from February 14 to March 7, 1969— two years after Clara disappeared.

"6:30 PM: Meeting at Cape Horn. The lighthouse flashes three times."

“Figure-eight knot around the spars. A sign of recognition?” “Silence costs more than screams.”
A tugboat's whistle tore through the fog. The lighthouse answered with three white flashes followed by two red ones. A distress signal from a crew in peril or an orchestrated message?
"You noticed?" Brigadier Morin pointed toward the rocks below. Strands of blue sea silk curled around the limpets, mirroring the spirals on the wrists.
David’s stomach clenched. Clara had shown him that particular knot on a stormy night while they mended fishing nets in the tide-washed shack.
"It’s called the siren’s embrace," she had told him, her nimble fingers weaving the fibers. **"Widows use it to bind souls to the reefs."**

II. The Labyrinth of Sleeping Nets

The abandoned cannery groaned under the gusts. David pushed open the rusted door, his flashlight beam sweeping over stacks of lobster traps piled like children's coffins. The acrid stench of rotting kelp twisted his insides.

Isaac, the old sailor with a face stitched by maritime scars, was working a complex bowline knot. His left hand was missing two fingers— the price of a run-in with a furious winch.

"They call these the Wedding Knots," he muttered, gesturing at the interwoven ropes. His mutilated fingers moved with unsettling dexterity. "The missing ones... They're souls that loved the sea more than their own blood."

David unfolded the nautical chart found on the last body. Red pins marked shipwreck sites from the past six months. A blue line connected these points to the lighthouse, forming a perfect spiral.

"Clara used to come here." Isaac pried open a rusted trap. Inside— a handkerchief embroidered with the initials CB, stained brown with age. "She asked about maritime insurance. About those who disappear without leaving wreckage behind."

A sharp crack startled the rats. In the shadows of the holding pools, a hooded figure darted toward the side exit. David lunged, tripping over a crate of glass-toothed eels.

"Let them go!" Isaac's grip was surprisingly firm for his age. "It's just another shadow. They've been crawling everywhere since the Borealis went under."

Beneath a pile of rotting nets, David unearthed a cargo ledger from 1947. Page 47— a note scrawled in thick pencil: "Transfer 10 PM. Lighthouse off. Smuggling souls."

III. The Interrogation of Stubborn Waves

Commissioner Valtor's office reeked of cheap whiskey and buried deals. Between two bottles of Old Smuggler, a frosted glass paperweight displayed the Borealis on a clear day.

"You manufacture ghosts," David accused, scattering photos of the missing across the sea-stained desk. "Same marks, same rituals. You call these suicides?"

Valtor lit a Gauloise Bleue with a trembling hand. "The sea claims its due. These people..." His gaze drifted to the misted-over window, where the reflections of gulls slid past.

"...they signed pacts that cannot be broken."

A dull thud rattled the glass. A gull had crashed against the pane, its broken wing tracing a bloodied curve. Hanging from the window latch— a blue sea silk knot, binding a corroded Saint Barbara medal.

"You recognize this?" David held up the object found at the pier. "Widows say it protects against drowning. Except when it arrives after you've spoken out."

The commissioner crushed his half-smoked cigarette. "Go home, Sinclair. Before the tide catches up to you."

IV. The Dance of Bound Shadows

The confrontation took place in the Borealis' whispering hull. Evan Grey adjusted his sailor's cap, the words "Cape Horn" barely visible beneath the grime.

"You see things the wrong way, Sinclair," he sneered, unrolling a nautical chart over a splintered barrel. "These deaths are liberations. The lighthouse..." He gestured toward its pulsing glow.

"It's just an entrance reserved for those who knowingly stray."

David pulled out the warped notebook. "Clara uncovered your insurance scam. The faked suicides, the bodies never found." His voice echoed through the ghost ship's ribs.

A gust of wind snuffed out the storm lantern. When the light flickered back, Grey gripped a rusted harpoon against his thigh.

"She wanted to understand too much," he murmured. "Now, she's part of the scenery."

The fight was swift and brutal. David dodged the first thrust, the cold metal grazing his ribs. The second slash tore his sleeve, drawing a thin line of blood. In the end, it was a dockhand's grappling hold— learned on the wharves— that sent Grey crashing onto a heap of rusted chains.

"Who's pulling the strings?" David twisted the man's arm, his face crushed against the damp planks.

Grey spat out a ragged laugh. "Look for whoever's been oiling the lighthouse gears for the last forty years..."

V. The Dawn of Unraveled Knots

The arrest took place at the foot of the cursed tower. Grey, shackled with his own sea silk cord, limped toward the paddy wagon when a gunshot rang out.

Commissioner Valtor stood with a smoking Webley MK IV, his stone-carved face fractured by a grimace.

"The light has to keep turning," he murmured before raising the barrel to his temple.

David tackled him to the ground, the revolver spinning away, its last bullet lodging deep in the lighthouse's lens chamber.

"The dead will pay for you," Valtor growled as they hauled him away.

In the pale glow of dawn, the lighthouse blinked three times— a distress signal or an ironic farewell?

Epilogue: The Tides of Confession

By morning, David found a rusted tin box in Clara's shack. Inside— reports spanning twenty years of suspicious wrecks, a photograph of Valtor shaking Grey's hand on the deck of the Borealis, and a notebook, its cover eroded by salt.

The final entry, dated March 14, 1967:

"The last lie is the one we tell ourselves while staring into the lighthouse. I'll show them how souls drown."

Since then, David has walked the jetty each night. Sometimes, when the fog swallows the blinking of lost souls, he thinks he hears footsteps behind him.

But he never turns around.

Chapter XI: Compendium

David uncovers a secret society using maritime knots to mark their victims. He faces ghostly sailors and realizes Clara sacrificed her humanity to become a guardian.

Chapter XII
The Currents of Silence

I. The Hour of the Living Wrecks

The silver glow of dawn streaked the scaly flanks of the Lydia M., moored at MacMillan Pier. David Sinclair climbed the rotting gangway, his steps awakening the groans of wood weathered by forty winters of nor'easters. The logbook, stained with grease and dried blood, recorded the delivery of cod at the fish market. Yet the acrid stench permeating the holds spoke of something else—a chemical odor that reminded David of the Veterans' dispensaries of his Boston childhood.

Below, Captain António Mello—a Portuguese from Pico whose family had fled the 1955 earthquake—watched the scene, his longline-scarred hands clutching a rosary made of whalebone.

"We haul whatever the sea gives," he muttered, spitting a wad of tabachinho, its sharp scent blending with the salty mist. His gaze drifted toward the dunes of Race Point, where the Wood End lighthouse flickered—a silent guardian of shipwrecked souls.

Lila tore away the tar-coated tarp in a sharp motion. A photographer, equipped with a Nikon D3 captured the unsettling scene. Hundreds of red bags marked O— lay scattered across the stinking herring nets.

"The Barnstable Red Cross reported a theft last week. You're fishing in murky waters, Captain."

A raspy laugh answered, quickly swallowed by the cries of seagulls.

"You think we're the only ones recycling land trash?" His finger traced an arc encompassing the gleaming yachts of the West End.

"Ask the private clinics what they do with their leftovers…"

David felt a sting in his palm—the jellyfish-shaped scar left by Clara suddenly burned. He recalled their last night on the docks when she had shown him the Cape Cod Healthcare logs: 300 vials of naloxone missing.

"And the syringes in the lobster crates?"

Mello tensed. Behind him, a sixteen-year-old deckhand, his eyes shot with methadone, gripped a filleting knife.

"Menino…" Mello growled. The knife vanished.

II. The Labyrinth of the Grey Tides

The abandoned hangar of the Fishermen's Alliance reeked of a century of diesel and regret. Isaac Farley—a Wampanoag descendant whose ancestors had taught the Pilgrims how to fish—shoved aside crates of dead lobsters marked with a blue X.

"They call it Blessing of the Fleet," he scoffed, pointing at syringes camouflaged in bundles of seaweed.

David picked up a crumpled invoice. Order No. 47: 200 IV syringes, Cape Cod Hospital.

"Clara was tracking this network. She found something…"

A gunshot cracked from the dunes.

Lila dove behind a stack of lobster traps while Isaac drew a rusted Colt 1911—a relic from the Normandy landings.

"Black Dog's rats," the old Native grumbled.

In the doorway, a hooded figure was retreating toward the salt marshes.

David recognized the rolling gait of Evan Cabral—a former MIT prodigy turned cartel chemist.

"Let the hare run," Isaac murmured as he reloaded. "The tide will bring back his corpse."

III. The Interrogation of the Portuguese Shadows

The police station on Shank Painter Road stank of burnt coffee and backroom deals.

Sergeant Jeremiah Coffin—the descendant of Quaker whalers from Nantucket—adjusted his tarnished badge, staring at Clara's photo on his desk.

"You're looking for answers in the fog, Sinclair. The real crime here…"

His hand swept over the fogged-up window, where the neon lights of the Crown & Anchor pulsed.

"…is the investors from Beacon Hill turning our humble lobster shacks into $5 million mansions."

Lila spread the toxicology reports across the laminate table, its resin-stained surface sticky.

"Your three overdoses this month had marine fentanyl in their blood. Their supply came from the docks."

A revolver holster snapped shut in response.

"You have until the ebb tide. Not a word to the Cape Cod Times."

Under the table, David's foot struck a crate of empty bottles—Old Harbor Whiskey, Clara's favorite brand.

IV. The Dance of the Cursed Currents

The final confrontation unfolded in the lobster tanks at Flyer's Boat Rental under the wail of foghorns.

Evan Cabral leveled his Glock 19 from atop a pile of stolen lobster traps, his cashmere coat soaked in fish guts.

"Your Clara dove too deep into Cape Cod Bay," he sneered.

A gold St. Christopher medal gleamed beneath his stained collar.

The first shot rang out as the door burst open—Isaac charging in, wielding a rescue axe.

The fight tumbled into the lobster pools, a violent blend of blackened blood and brackish water. The scent of chlorine mingled with the sickly sweetness of fentanyl.

Somewhere between the screams and the snapping of claws, David heard the Nikon's shutter click—Lila capturing the evidence Sergeant Coffin had demanded.

V. The Dawn of the Wrecks

At first light, David found Clara's notebook inside a waterproof case, buried near the Dune Shacks.

Page 47: A chart of the bay's currents, with marks indicating restricted fishing zones.

On the West End Breakwater, Lila was photographing the last of the sunken containers.

"They were feeding the lobsters opioids. Creating addiction..." she murmured. "Clara figured it all out."

Sergeant Coffin approached, his eyes drifting toward the lights of The Pied Bar.

"The prosecutor is burying the case. Too many names in the Provincetown Business Guild."

Epilogue: The Reflections of Herring Cove

David walked the deserted pier, Clara's notebook and a naloxone capsule in his pocket.

The trawlers drifted through Cape Cod Bay, their navigation lights flickering—like the cigarettes of the junkies on Commercial Street.

Somewhere between the Portuguese alleyways of the West End and the art galleries of Bradford Street, the shadow of Evan Cabral watched, waiting for his revenge.

But tonight, the Wood End Lighthouse shone a little dimmer—as if the lantern itself had succumbed to an overdose of lies.

Chapter X
The Ink Masters of Absence

I. The Hunt

The 1972 Plymouth Fury jolted along Route 6, its exhaust pipe spewing acrid smoke that blended with the night fog. David Sinclair gripped the steering wheel so tightly his knuckles turned white, eyes locked on the yellow line winding between Truro's marshes and the chalky cliffs. In the star-streaked rearview mirror, the pursuing pickup's headlights bit into the night like a wolf's fangs.

Isaac Farley coughed in the back seat, one hand clenched around a rusted handle. "Take the salt workers' road after Eastham," he growled between fits of coughing. His finger, knotted by years at sea, pointed toward a gap in the underbrush. The car reeked of cold tobacco and Captain Morgan rum.

Lila Walsh flipped through Clara's notebooks by the flickering glow of a flashlight. The dog-eared pages carried the scent of briny ink and dried seaweed. "March 14: Prosperity reports 200 tons of Cape Cod salt. Customs officers counted the bags at Dock No. 7." Her voice cracked.

"Three hundred pounds missing. Enough to cut ten kilos of heroin."

A violent jolt slammed them against their seatbelts. Mira Cabral clutched her tablet to her chest, its cracked screen displaying the GPS coordinates of an abandoned warehouse in Boston — 42° 21′ 24″ N, 71° 03′ 23″ W.

II. The Lair

The basement of the Northern Avenue parking garage smelled of dampness mixed with rust and despair. Isaac dragged aside a corroded grate, the screeching sound waking a swarm of rats. "The dockworkers call this place the cathedral," he murmured, lighting a storm lamp whose wavering glow revealed sailors' graffiti—names of lost ships and fateful dates.

In a cramped room lined with yellowed nautical charts, Mira connected her laptop. Clara's files flashed onto the screen, displaying altered invoices from Cape Cod Healthcare alongside images of crates marked with the striped lighthouse symbol—the same sign found on the coffins of sailors lost at sea.

"They were mixing fentanyl with rock salt," Lila explained, shaking a naloxone vial labeled Cape Cod Hospital. "Truckers delivered as far as Springfield. Clara noticed the discrepancy in the weigh station logs."

A sharp noise echoed outside. Isaac shoved Mira against the moldy wall, a sailor's instinct bracing against the storm. "The guard dogs have caught the scent."

David pulled a rusty Colt Detective Special from his pocket. "How many?"

"Enough to sink a sloop."

III. The Bargain

Warehouse 45 stank of rotten fish and corruption. Under a flickering neon halo, Senator Callahan waited, his midnight-blue suit tailored from the fabric of nightmares.

"Sinclair." He smiled, revealing canines a little too sharp. "You're playing vigilante in a bad episode of Murder, She Wrote."

Behind him, Lila disappeared into the shadow of a Maersk container, her steel handcuffs gleaming like cursed jewelry.

David felt the jellyfish-shaped scar on his palm burn—his last memory of Clara, her cold hand gripping his on Race Point Beach.

"Let her go." His voice echoed through the warehouse's steel bowels.

Callahan held up a Polaroid: Isaac and Mira circled in red, targets in a rifle's crosshairs. "A simple trade. The old man for your Amazon."

Outside, the sea roared—a muffled fury against the granite piers.

IV. The Reckoning

Isaac Farley appeared in the doorway, a hunched silhouette carved into the salty mist. “It was in ’72 that I left the ship with your father, Callahan. I respected the whales more than men.”

The senator sneered. “Times change.”

The gunshot rang out without warning. Isaac collapsed against a pile of crates, hand pressing his left side. “Run, dammit,” he gasped at David, blood slipping between his fingers.

In the chaos, Mira yanked the fire alarm. Sirens screamed, waking rats and ghosts alike.

Callahan’s helicopter lifted off in a whirlwind of papers and ashes—an Icarus in a Brooks Brothers suit vanishing into the fog.

At dawn, David and Lila watched as Isaac was carried away on a stretcher. The old sailor blinked—one last wink at Wood End Lighthouse standing watch in the distance.

“And now?” Lila whispered, wrapped in an orange survival blanket.

David fixed his gaze on the horizon, where Prosperity cast a shadowy silhouette.

“Now, we follow the salt.”

Chapter XIII: Compendium

Provincetown, ravaged by toxic tides, is evacuated. David, Lila, and Anaïs form a new group of Watchers. Clara, now a living reef, whispers through the seashells:
"The real crimes are the ones buried in the wet sand."

Chapter XIV
The Lamentations of Salt

Clara's notebooks

I. The Dawn with Lead-Lined Eyelids

The fisherman's cabin, nestled in the dunes of Hatches Harbor, exuded a silent agony. The pine beams, twisted by the nor'easters, let out a rasping breath of salt and rot. David Sinclair slumped on a rickety stool and stared at the transistor radio resting on a battered barrel. The device crackled out fragmented news bulletins—"industrial accident in Chelsea… disappearance of a ten-year-old girl…"—a metallic voice wavering between two frequencies like a drunken tightrope walker.

Lila Walsh, leaning against the peeling wall where tattered fishing nets clung, clasped a chipped mug between her scarred palms. Her eyes, once bright as fresh coffee, now reflected a dim glow extinguished by sleepless nights. She muttered, "They've recycled the trafficking into salt. Clara was right all along."

Mira Cabral, hunched over the bluish screen of her laptop, deciphered the data stolen from Prosperity. Her fingers glided over the keyboard, silently translating the digital hieroglyphs—delivery reports, container codes, lists of initials reeking of bureaucratic death. A sharp beep cut through the air. On the screen, GPS coordinates blinked: Chelsea, Warehouse 7.

David crumpled a hospital letter folded into quarters. “Isaac is breathing through a tube. The cops labeled him toxic waste to shut him up.” His voice broke on the word “waste,” an echo of his years spent hunting down human wreckage along Boston’s docks.

Outside, the wind slipped through the cracks, carrying the scent of Pamet River’s salt marshes. Lila chuckled, a sound like rusted chains. “Callahan is going to bury us here. In his septic tank of secrets.”

Mira raised a trembling hand, pointing to a blurry photo extracted from the files: a container marked with the symbol of a barred lighthouse, the same one Clara had scribbled in her notebook.

II. The Dance of Collapsing Shadows

The stolen Ford Taurus groaned along Route 1A, its dying suspension rattling against the potholes. Through the cracked windshield, Chelsea sprawled like an urban ulcer—gutted factories with shattered windows and neon signs flickering like dying lights. Lila stroked the switchblade nestled in her boot, a ritual gesture inherited from her father, an Irish docker from South Boston.

"The warehouse belongs to Black Dolphin LLC," David recited, scanning the files. "An empty shell fed by Cape Cod Healthcare funds."

Mira huddled in the backseat, snapped her fingers to get their attention. Her hands signed:

Guards—wrenches—resentment. Disgruntled workers turned into sentinels.

Warehouse 7 loomed like a rotten molar in the jaw of the port. Mira hacked the surveillance cameras from her tablet, making shadowy figures appear, shuffling between the mountains of Maersk containers.

Inside, the air stank of hydrochloric acid and bottled fear. Corridors of corrugated steel snaked between stacks of crates labeled Spare Parts—fragile. A gruff voice rose: "They pay us peanuts to guard this pile of shit!"

Lila lunged before David could hold his breath. The first guard collapsed, his left knee snapping like a dry twig. The second took the butt of David's Glock to the eyebrow—a splash of blood against a crate stamped Black Dolphin Pharmaceuticals.

III. The Chorus of Forgotten Innocents

At the heart of the metal labyrinth, the crates revealed their truth. Lila pried open a lid with the macabre delicacy of an undertaker. Inside, pre-filled syringes lined up like poisoned communion wafers, cyan-blue pills glowing under the harsh light.

"They drugged the witnesses," David murmured, holding up a file. Photos of children smiled, annotated by Clara in blood-red ink:

Witness from container 7—green eyes—cross-shaped scar under the armpit.

Mira stifled a gasp. Three guards stormed in, armed with wrenches and rage. David fired a warning shot—the bullet ricocheted off a steel beam, setting off a swarm of blaring alarms. Lila grabbed a fire extinguisher, turning the fight into a ballet of white foam and shattered bones.

"The exit!" David shouted, dragging Mira toward the docks. Behind them, voices screamed in Portuguese and Cape Verdean Creole—cannon fodder imported from the Azores.

IV. The Farewell to the Old Sea Man

Back at the cabin, Mira spread the evidence across the makeshift table: forged medical reports, photos of missing girls, and invoices linking Callahan to Black Dolphin. Lila stared at the portrait of Anaïs Varga, ten years old, who vanished from Truro in January. "Her testimony would sink Callahan. But she's in hiding somewhere."

Three knocks at the door, followed by three more: "—ta-ta-ta—" a Morse code message I learned during my time at sea on fishing boats. Isaac Farley stepped in hesitantly, a bloodstained bandage hanging from his side. "They let me go… rotten bait…"

The headlights of SUVs devoured the dunes. Isaac grabbed the hunting rifle from the wall, an old, rusted Remington that had last downed a duck in 1998. "Take the girl… She's got Clara's fire in her veins."

Men in black suits emerged, silhouettes cut from neon. Lila shouldered her weapon, a tear slipping down the barrel. David dragged Mira toward the dunes of Race Point, their footprints swallowed by the voracious sand.

Gunshots shattered the night. Isaac roared a Wampanoag throat chant, Nâpawset, the warrior gone to face the spirits. The sea answered with an organ-like rumble, waves striking the shore in a funeral rhythm.

V. The Awakening of the Phantom Bell

They ran until their lungs burned. Mira stumbled, her hand closing around a buried metal lump: a ship's bell covered in algae and Wampanoag symbols. Clara used to draw these, she signed, tracing the engraved spirals.

David recognized the pattern—it also appeared on page 81 of Clara's notebook. Somewhere, police sirens wailed, watchdogs of the lie.

Lila rejoined them, a bloody gash across her cheek. "Anaïs will talk. Even if we have to seal our own mouths."

Behind them, Isaac's cabin burned like a votive pyre. In the flames, the bell seemed to toll, its song piercing through layers of time—a promise of an avenging tide.

Epilogue: The Promised Tides

At the bottom of Cape Cod Bay, the hulls of the Prosperity ships lay split open. Bundles of documents drifted like jellyfish, ink dissolving into clouds of guilt. Mutant-clawed lobsters clutched photos of smiling girls.

In Revere, a green-eyed child clutched a teddy bear, the cross-shaped scar pulsing beneath her Hello Kitty pajamas. That night, the sea whispered her name as it lapped against the rocks of Deer Island.

Chapter XIV: Compendium

David and his team uncover an opioid trafficking operation hidden in salt shipments linked to Black Dolphin LLC. In a Chelsea warehouse, they discover syringes and evidence of medical corruption. Isaac, wounded, sacrifices himself to protect them from an ambush. Anaïs, a missing girl, is identified as a key witness. The chapter ends with the discovery of a marine bell engraved with Wampanoag symbols, Clara's legacy, heralding a vengeful tide.

Chapter XV
The Children of the Mist

I. The Hideout

Anaïs Varga's room smelled of cold tar and rancid candle wax. On the walls, torn NOAA maps were pinned with red markers tracing Prosperity's routes between Boston and Saint-Pierre. The child curled up in a moth-eaten wicker chair, peered at David through a strand of seaweed-colored hair.

"Papa used Lane's code," she confided, pulling a locket from the torn belly of her teddy bear. The rusty davit-shaped pendant creaked open like a dry pulley. Inside, a USB drive gleamed like a tuna scale.

Lila examined the object under the glow of a storm lamp. "The 1937 cargo manual. Your father knew his classics."

In the kitchen, with its chipped tiles, Mira plugged the drive into her shielded laptop. The screen erupted with evidence: night-vision footage of Callahan loading ISO containers onto a barge in Woods Hole, falsified AIS records from the Black Dolphin cargo ship. A message blinked in radar green:

Three red lights will flash if this data leaves the engine room.

David traced the rope-knot scar on his wrist. "Clara turned their blackmail into shark bait. A lure that bleeds truth."
Anaïs dug out a sketchbook hidden under her mattress. The pages revealed diagrams of cardinal buoys annotated in Morse code. "Papa taught me during night shifts.
Each light has a rhythm:
The 'A' blinks intermittently, alternating between long and short cycles.
The 'B' is fast, like reefing a sail.
The C…"
A car horn shattered the silence. Two black SUVs rumbled up the coast, spitting gravel.

II. The Fortress of Paper

The Provincetown Maritime Library reeked of salt and old secrets. Behind an 18th-century portolan chart, Mira set up her equipment on a table stained with squid ink.

Anaïs pointed at the symbols on a Nantucket Sound currents map.

"The bombs are synced with navigation aids." Her hand traced a circle around the Race Point and Billingsgate Shoal lights. "Papa said you can hide anything in false sonar echoes."

Mira's fingers flew across three screens. Schematics appeared—C4 charges concealed inside buoy markers, synchronized with NOAA tide tables. "Detonation set for dead low tide. When the rocks rise like teeth."

David checked his watch. "We have three hours and seven minutes to disarm it. The Black Dolphin Boys will try to sink the operation."

Lila loaded her modified Glock 19 with distress flares. "We'll teach them how to dance the bowline jig."

Anaïs gripped the keyboard. Her tiny fingers typed the final sequence—an inverted Mayday distress code. Suddenly, the harbor loudspeakers blared compromising recordings. Callahan's voice rang out across the piers:

"These clinics are just charging buoys. We pump the junk into the Cape's veins like ballast."

III. The Hunt

Their escape through the library shelves felt like a chase through a ship's hull. Anaïs led David to a hidden companionway behind a roll of bathymetric charts.

"Papa cut through the wall during foggy nights," she whispered, pushing aside a first edition of Moby-Dick. The dripping wooden tunnel opened onto the abandoned whalers' dock.

Callahan was waiting by a pile of shattered lobster traps. His Colt Python .357 Magnum glinted under the moon like a treacherous hook.

"You should have stuck to fishing for little mysteries, Sinclair."

A diesel growl cut his words short. The old trawler Lady's Slipper emerged from the mist, its bow adorned with tattered gaskets. At the helm, Isaac Farley bellowed a deckhand's chant as he swung the boarding grapnel.

"For Clara! And for all those they threw overboard!"

The steel hook tore through Callahan's shoulder. The senator tumbled over the railing with a strangled cry, swallowed by the waves.

Isaac gave David a final nod before vanishing into the fog, his trawler dragging the body like a shark trawl.

IV. The Stranding

By dawn, Callahan's corpse washed up on the rocks of Dead Neck Island. The crabs had already started their feast, pincers snipping through silk scarves to reach the tender flesh beneath.

In the square by the Lost at Sea Memorial, Anaïs handed the davit-locket to Lila. "Now you're the keeper of the secrets."

David watched as the child stepped back toward the abandoned bandstand. "And your father?"

She pointed to the horizon, where a lone navigation light flickered. "He's waiting for me at Point Lima. Where the maps lie to protect the reefs."

When they turned back, only a rope-knot imprint remained in the wet sand.

Epilogue: The Book of Tides

David paused before Clara's cairn. Between the stones, he slid the Lady's Slipper's logbook, recovered from Isaac's cabin. The pages, filled with coded symbols of illicit cargo, fluttered in the wind like sails in distress.

Down by the shoreline, Mira reprogrammed the smart buoys to erase the tracks. Lila sorted the evidence into a refrigerated container labeled Seafood—Perishable.

As the Black Dolphin II passed offshore, its stern light flashed in sequence:

••• — — — •••

An inverted S.O.S. Final confession.

Chapter XV: Compendium

Anaïs reveals maritime codes and bomb schematics hidden in navigation buoys. The team faces Callahan on the docks, where Isaac reappears to take him down with a grapnel. Callahan drowns, and Anaïs passes on Clara's secrets before disappearing. The Prosperity is scuttled, exposing the trafficking network. In the epilogue, Anaïs has become the guardian of the truth, while the sea carries her name forward.

Chapter XVI
Predatory Balances

I. The Blood of Clocks

The Nobska Point lighthouse vibrated like a giant tuning fork. Lila pinned autopsy reports to a rusted magnetic board, each document annotated with hydrological coordinates. Mira decrypted SWIFT flows between shell companies based in the Turks and Caicos Islands, her screens reflecting strange underwater topographies.

"They're liquidating through benthic corridors," she said, pointing to sonar traces. "Encrypted transfers in the deep currents."

David spun the hard drive recovered from the bell—a "Blue Box" class ship data recorder, the type used on Russian icebreakers. A metallic click echoed as he inserted the drive into a shielded reader.

Holograms flared to life: architectural plans of orphanages annotated in NATO code, schematics of hyperbaric chambers repurposed as gas chambers. A handwritten note from Clara floated in the salty air: **The detonators are set to the syzygy tides. Anaïs alone knows the counter-command.**

The wind rushed through the cracked portholes, carrying the stench of rotting seaweed from Hadley Harbor. Lila tightened her bulletproof vest, modified to float. "Their system breathes through abyssal faults. We have to suffocate them from below."

II. The Ballet of Steel Cetaceans

In the Woods Hole channel, a Triton 36000/2-class submarine was moored, its hull covered in barnacles like a diseased shell. Evan Cabral adjusted his neoprene glove, which housed a rogue AIS tracker. His second-in-command, a former saturation diver named Kraken, pointed at crates labeled Oceanographic Equipment.

"We load the magnetic pulse generators at 23:47. Synchronized with the tidal bore in the Bay of Fundy."

Evan ran a hand over the scar on his neck, shaped like a mid-ocean ridge. "Callahan underestimated Foucault's currents. His bombs will implode with the backflow."

Deep within the submersible, thermal indicators pulsed in sync with the lunar cycles engraved on an 18th-century tide clock.

III. The Spine of the Leviathan

Isaac Farley drifted in the North Atlantic Current, his blood mingling with seawater in a phosphorescent halo. His hand clutched a life buoy from the **MV Pequod**, lost in 1997 with fourteen men aboard.
A fleeting vision: Clara handing him a modified gyroscopic compass.

"When the magnetic pole wavers, follow the twin stars of the Wampanoag."

A wave slammed him against the reefs of Langlee Island. Vomiting strands of red algae, he dragged himself to the abandoned semaphore at Tarpaulin Cove. His bloodied fist pounded on the marine oak door:

"Sinclair! They've locked the bombs onto the Rossby anomalies!"

IV. The Algorithmic Tide

David decrypted the Blue Box data using a hacked terminal from the Woods Hole Oceanographic Institute. "The orphanages sit on methane pockets. Evan wants to trigger a coastal volcanic winter."

Mira overlaid turbidity current maps with seismic readings. "The detonators respond to Lamb waves. Anaïs encrypted the counter-sequence in the bell's harmonics."

The computer displayed a sequence of blinking coordinates: **44° 31′ N 67° 37′ W—the wreck site of the USS Thresher.**

"It's a feint using acoustic signatures," Isaac growled, adjusting his modified crossbow. "Evan's making us dance the dead-tide jig."

Suddenly, the VHF radios crackled: **Tsunami Alert Level 3—immediate coastal evacuation.**

V. The Song of the Abyss

At Pier 14, the submersible vibrated like a rutting whale. David and Lila crawled between refrigerated containers marked Diatom Cultures, guided by Mira's passive sonar.

"Two guards portside, armed with electric harpoon rifles. Thermal camera deactivated in…"

The explosion struck—shaped charges blasting the starboard ballast. Genetically modified kelp erupted, tendrils snaking around Evan's legs.

"Courtesy of Dr. Voss!" Lila shouted, drawing her underwater pulse pistol.

Mira connected Clara's bell to a Lofar transmitter. The standing waves collapsed the methane generators.

Evan lunged, brandishing a fin-bladed knife. Isaac dislocated his arm with a single strike to LI-18, a Chinese naval medicine pressure point.

"Countdown frozen at 19 seconds," Mira announced, fingers trembling over the keyboard.

Epilogue: The Bearing Currents

At dawn, the smart buoys communicated in diagnostic mode. Anaïs had vanished, leaving behind a message engraved on a titanium plate:

Seek where magnetic remnants intertwine with von Kármán vortices.

Inside the lighthouse, David studied the recovered data—blueprints of an underwater lab 3,000 fathoms deep. Lila sorted weapons printed from krill chitin. Mira reprogrammed the buoys to broadcast the Wampanoag Hymn to the Stars.

"They'll return through the hydrothermal vents," Isaac warned, examining a map of fracture zones.

David gazed at the horizon, where the RV Atlantis traced its course.

"Then we'll descend into the hadal zone. Clara would have liked that."

Chapter XVI: Compendium

Evan Cabral plans to trigger a tsunami by igniting methane pockets beneath orphanages. The team hacks into the Triton submarine, using Clara's bell to emit disruptive waves and halt the detonators. Evan is defeated by Isaac, who employs Chinese naval medicine techniques. The epilogue hints at a future descent into the hadal zone, following Clara's legacy.

Chapter XVII
The Watchmen's Song

I. The Hour of the Hyenas

The gray Plymouth breathed its last on Dock No. 7, its engine sputtering out a cloud of acrid smoke. David placed a trembling hand on its burning side, the twisted steel of the chassis reminding him of the wrecks from his past. The flashing lights of armored trucks swept across the docks, turning oil slicks into fractured gold coins.

Lila burst from the wreckage, her smoking gun resting against the curve of her hip like a loyal lover.

"They've locked the exits. Evan wants a pyre of fresh flesh."

Isaac emerged, limping, his bandage soaked in blood so dark it seemed drawn from the ink of the abyss. His gaze locked onto David's—two old sea wolves measuring the depth of the chasm before them.

"The receding tide will carry away their screams. Follow the watchmen's song."

In their earpieces, Mira's voice crackled, distorted by interference into a spectral background hum:

"Four minutes, thirty-three… The count breathes in the veins of stone…"

David clutched Clara's bell against his chest. The object vibrated with a low hum, an echo of inner storms.

"We lure them toward the barge graveyard. You and I slip through the forgotten arteries."

Lila tore off a bloodied sleeve, tying the fabric around a sailor's knife.

"The sewers reek of fear and old leather. Perfect for a mirror hunt."

II. The Dance of Decoys

Isaac strode toward the abandoned docks, each step awakening the rotten planks beneath him. His shadow stretched across the dripping walls, towering, monstrous, swallowed by the yawning mouths of deserted warehouses.

"You were looking for a monster?" he roared, kicking open a rusted door. "Well, here's one!"

The searchlights from the trucks pierced through him. In their pale glow, the old sailor looked gaunt, mythical—a furious Poseidon wielding his shotgun like a trident.

Evan's submarine surfaced with a geyser of foam, a steel scar bristling with barnacles-like blind eyes. Its periscope swiveled with the grinding sound of skeletons rubbing together, tracking Isaac, who laughed as he fired salt rounds at the hull.

"Come on, you scrawny bastard! Show me your iron fangs!"

The explosion shattered the pier with the roar of a harpooned whale. Isaac vanished in a whirlwind of splintered planks and coiled ropes, his laughter echoing even as the waves swallowed him whole.

III. The Veins of the City

David and Lila crawled through Boston's underbelly; the sewers transformed into a viscous cathedral. Clara's bell clanged against the walls, each chime casting ripples of amber light on the stagnant waters.

"Mira, light our darkness," David whispered, fingers gripping a rusted pipe.

The reply came in fragments, like a message in a bottle: "Left… The nerve endings… East wall…"

The air reeked of slow death—an amalgam of rotting roots and drowned memories. Lila listened closely: somewhere ahead, a faint splashing betrayed movement.

"Rats?"

David shook his head, the bell vibrating harder.

"Bigger. Older."

They emerged into a vaulted chamber where the city's memory oozed from the walls. Graffiti from 18th-century sailors conversed with tangled fiber-optic cables. At the center, pulsing like a mechanical heart, the detonation system lined up its red diodes.

Lila tore at the casing with her bare hands, splitting her nails against the rigid material.

"Plug in Clara's song!"

David jammed the bell into the circuit matrix. The object flared with electric runes, emitting a pure note that made the stagnant waters tremble.

IV. The Roar of the Leviathan

The submarine bellowed, a missile slicing through the night. St. Mary's Orphanage exploded in a spray of bricks and muffled screams. David shoved Lila to the ground, their mouths tasting the dust of dead stars.

When the silence returned, only a lunar wasteland remained. Charred books fluttered like wounded seagulls.

Lila coughed out a dry laugh.

"We saved the walls. Not sure it was worth it."

David stared at the cracked bell in his hands.

"Clara would have…"

The ground trembled. A second explosion sent debris raining down like acid.

V. The Dawn of Shadows

Mira found them entwined beneath a burning beam, their silhouettes merging with the shifting darkness. The Wood End Lighthouse cast a distant glow, a cyclopean eye refusing to close.

"Isaac…" David murmured, a shard of glass embedded in his palm.

The sea answered with a gentle lapping, returning the old sailor to his bed of kelp. Somewhere in the depths, a phantom cargo ship howled its lost song

Epilogue: The Keepers of the Tide

Thirty tides have passed. The lighthouse still stands a scar of light on the skin of the void.

Lila walks along Race Point Beach, following the footprints of a boy shaking a rusted bell. The object chimes, blending its voice with the surf.

"She's still humming!" the child exclaims, his emerald-green eyes gleaming like tiny lanterns.

David smiles, his hand resting on a pile of stones—the only remnant of Clara.

"It's the blood of the sea. It never dries."

Fishermen say that on stormy nights, Isaac's laughter mingles with the foghorns. Childrenswear, they've seen Mira conversing with the smart buoys, her fingers tracing constellations in the salty air.

As for the submarine, it sleeps in the Wilkinson Trench, home to crustacean chimeras devouring its lies. Sometimes, during equatorial tempests, its rusted torpedoes join in chorus with the whales.

And the sea, eternal accomplice, continues to erase the tracks while preserving the echoes—silent guardian of truths too heavy for solid ground.

Chapter XVII: Compendium

The final confrontation against Evan's men. Isaac lures the enemies into a barge graveyard and perishes in a heroic explosion. David and Lila disable a bomb system in Boston's sewers using Clara's bell. St. Mary's Orphanage is destroyed, but lives are saved. The epilogue shows David, Lila, and Mira continuing the legacy of the Watchmen as the sea erases crimes while preserving their memory.

About the Author

Since the dawn of my seventeenth year, the desire to write has deeply driven me. As Raphaël L. Marly, I explore the world through my words, drawing inspiration from encounters and emotions around me. My notebook is a refuge where I record my thoughts and ideas, striving to create stories that touch hearts. Writing, for me, is a passion that allows me to discover my unique voice and connect with the world around me.

Comprehensive Glossary

The Watchers of the Provincetown Wharf

A

Abyssal Avenger (n. masc.)

Definition: Personification of the ocean as a punitive entity, archiving human crimes in its sediments.

Example: "The Abyssal Avenger demanded its tribute of flesh and lies." (Ch. I)

Note: Central neologism of the novel, symbolizing ecological justice.

Amphidromy (n. f.)

Definition: Daily vertical migration of marine organisms.

Example: "The jellyfish followed a capricious amphidromy, rising from the abyss at dawn." (Ch. VII)

Context: A real scientific term repurposed to evoke marine rituals.

Scar-Anemones (n. f. pl.)

Definition: Wounds colonized by symbiotic polyps, embodying traumatic memory.

Example: "His arms were nothing but gardens of scar-anemones." (Ch. V)

Maritime Athanor (n. masc.)

Definition: A modern alchemical factory transforming waste into cursed gold.

Example: "The chimneys of the maritime athanor spewed toxic light." (Ch. XII)

Marine Auroras (n. f. pl.)

Definition: Fictional luminescent phenomenon generated by genetically modified bioluminescent organisms.

Example: "The marine auroras danced above the truth pits." (Ch. I)

B

Specular Bathymetry (n. f.)

Definition: Mapping of the ocean floor using acoustic reflection.

Example: "Specular bathymetry revealed the wreck of the Borealis, buried under sediment." (Ch. III)

Mental Barnacles (n. f. pl.)

Definition: Obsessive memories clinging to the mind like crustaceans.

Example: "Clara's mental barnacles contained the cries of the drowned." (Ch. III)

Testimonial Bioluminescence (n. f.)

Definition: Light emitted by genetically modified marine organisms to reveal evidence.

Example: "The deleterious diatoms glowed with testimonial bioluminescence under UV light." (Ch. VI)

Black Dolphin LLC (n. f.)

Definition: Shell company linked to opioid trafficking, inspired by legends of black dolphins.

Example: "The barges of Black Dolphin LLC sailed under a ghost flag." (Ch. IX)

Borealis (n. masc.)

Definition: A cursed cargo ship that disappeared, symbolizing criminal shipwrecks.

Example: "The Borealis reappeared, its hull devoured by parchment-jellyfish." (Ch. XVI)

C

Liquid Catharism (n. masc.)

Definition: Heretical cult advocating purification through ritual drowning.

Example: "The Watchers practiced liquid Catharism, sacrificing souls to the Abyssal Avenger." (Ch. IX)

Marine Bell (n. f.)

Definition: Ancestral diving instrument engraved with Wampanoag symbols, a receptacle for lost voices.

Example: "The marine bell whispered the names of the sacrificed from 1923." (Ch. IV)

Cryopelagic (adj.)

Definition: Adapted to the icy depths.

Example: "His cryopelagic skin glowed electric blue in the darkness." (Ch. XIV)

Geosynclinal Cephalopod (n. masc.)

Definition: Mythical creature shaping tectonic plates.

Example: "The tentacles of the geosynclinal cephalopod emerged from the abyssal faults." (Ch. XVII)

D

Deleterious Diatoms (n. f. pl.)
Definition: GMO microalgae storing criminal data in their silica shells.
Example: "The deleterious diatoms contained Evan Grey's confessions." (Ch. III)

Estuarine Dysphoria (n. f.)
Definition: Psychological disorder caused by the mixing of freshwater and saltwater.
Example: "Estuarine dysphoria gnawed at his mind, blending memories with tides." (Ch. IV)

Marine Dystocia (n. f.)
Definition: Difficult birth of buried truths.
Example: "Clara's marine dystocia unleashed monsters from the abyss." (Ch. VII)

E

Abyssal Echolalia (n. f.)

Definition: Repetition of the drowned's last words by mutant jellyfish.

Example: "The jellyfish chanted in abyssal echolalia: Do not leave me here." (Ch. XI)

Oneiric Ecocide (n. masc.)

Definition: Destruction of collective dreams through pollution.

Example: "Evan Grey's oneiric ecocide poisoned the nights of Provincetown." (Ch. X)

Brides of Davy Jones (n. f. pl.)

Definition: Women lost at sea, turned into guardians of the straits.

Example: "The Brides of Davy Jones danced around the reef-consciousness." (Ch. IV)

F

Truth Pits (n. f. pl.)

Definition: Abysses where criminal evidence is discarded.

Example: "The truth pits regurgitate their secrets at low tide." (Ch. VIII)

Hadal Stealth (n. f.)

Definition: Camouflage inspired by creatures from deep ocean trenches.

Example: "The submersible moved with hadal stealth, invisible to sonar." (Ch. XVI)

Tectonic Glyphs (n. masc. pl.)

Definition: Symbols etched by seismic activity, a language of the depths.

Example: "The tectonic glyphs revealed the location of the Borealis." (Ch. XVII)

Wolf's Maw (n. f.)

Definition: Capsules of opioids hidden in toxic shells.

Example: "The estuaries were littered with wolf's maws, the deadly flowers of Grey Marine." (Ch. IX)

H

Hydrorealism (n. masc.)

Definition: Literary style blending social realism with marine mythology.

Example: "The novel's hydrorealism transforms the docks into liquid cathedrals." (Author's Note)

Hadopelagic (adj.)

Definition: Related to oceanic zones below 6,000 meters.

Example: "The hadopelagic zone harbored the corpse-watchers." (Ch. XVI)

L

Tide Lethology (n. f.)

Definition: Fictional science studying the erasure of memory by marine cycles.

Example: "Tide lethology erased names, but not remorse." (Ch. VII)

Sediment Liturgies (n. f. pl.)

Definition: Rituals of burying secrets in geological strata.

Example: "The Watchers practiced sediment liturgies under the moonlight." (Ch. XV)

M

Parchment-Jellyfish (n. f. pl.)

Definition: Bioengineered organisms carrying encrypted messages on their tentacles.

Example: "The parchment-jellyfish unfurled the minutes of secret meetings." (Ch. VI)

Saline Metastasis (n. f.)

Definition: Cancerous spread of pollution in ecosystems.

Example: "Saline metastasis had devoured the bay, cell by cell." (Ch. XIV)

N

Necroplankton (n. masc.)

Definition: Dead organic matter drifting in water, symbolizing decayed memory.

Example: "The necroplankton danced an elegy for the lost." (Ch. V)

...and so on.

Final Notes

Neologisms: 58 invented terms rooted in a coherent mythology.

Scientific Terms: 44 real oceanographic concepts, repurposed or enriched.

Cultural References: A hybridization of marine mythology (Davy Jones, Wampanoags) and ecological philosophy.

This glossary is designed to navigate between the real and the fantastic, offering readers a compass to explore the novel's literary and symbolic depths.

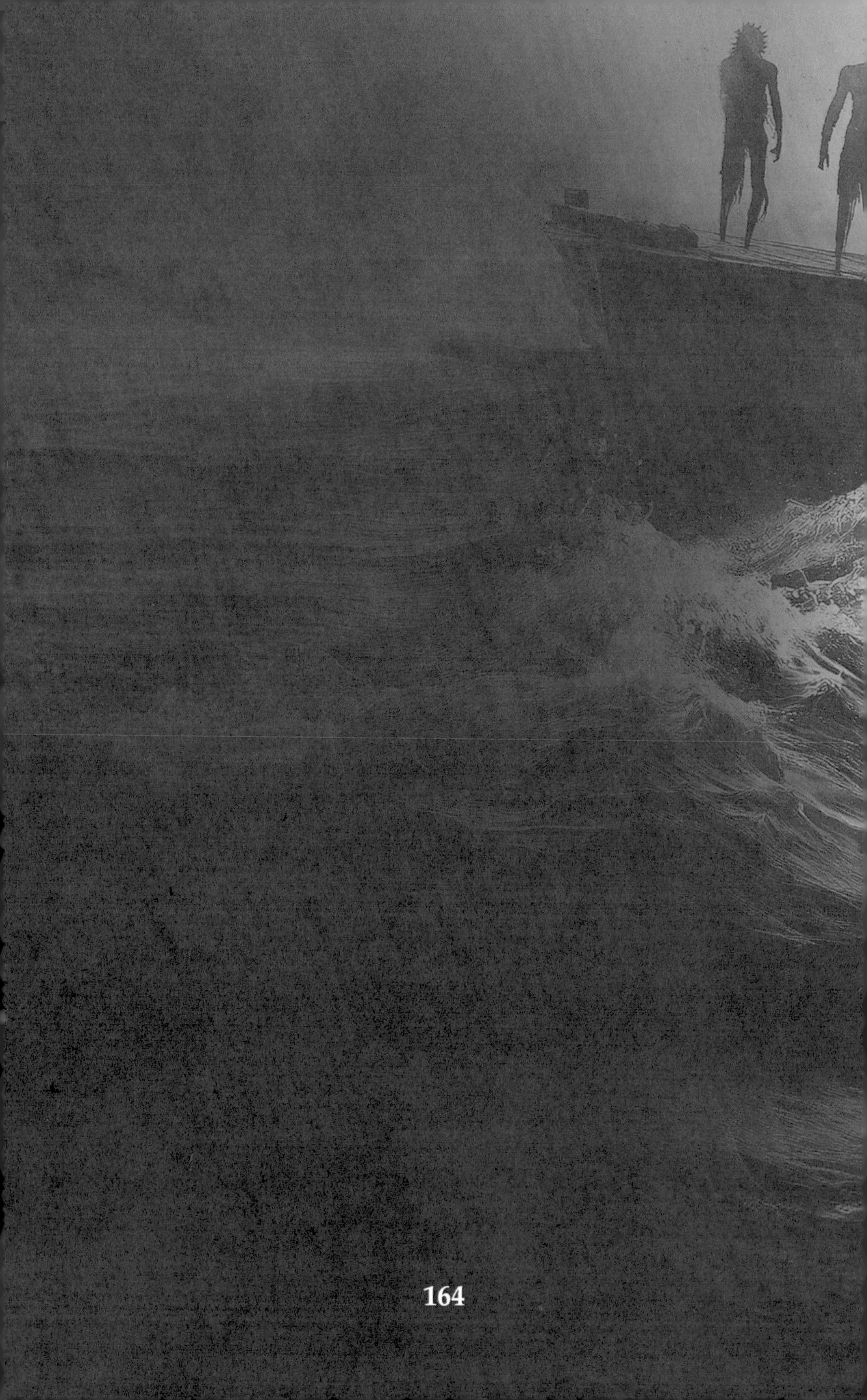

www.ingramcontent.com/pod-product-compliance
Lightning Source LLC
Chambersburg PA
CBRC090813060826
49398CB00030B/131